Also by David Michael Williams

TALES OF ALTAERRA

Magic's Daughter

The Renegade Chronicles

Rebels and Fools

Heroes and Liars

Martyrs and Monsters

THE SOUL SLEEP CYCLE

If Souls Can Sleep

If Sin Dwells Deep

If Dreams Can Die

STANDALONE

The Lost Tale of Sir Larpsalot

Ghost Mode

&

Other Strange Stories

David Michael Williams

ONEMILLIONWORDS

Ghost Mode & Other Strange Stories is a work of fiction.
Names, characters, places, and incidents either are products of the
author's imagination or are used fictitiously. Any resemblance to
actual persons, living or dead, business establishments, events, or
locales is entirely coincidental.

ONEMILLIONWORDS

First published by One Million Words, LLC, Wisconsin, USA

First printing, June 2021

ISBN 978-1-7322117-9-7

Written by David Michael Williams (david-michael-williams.com)

Cover art copyright © 2021 by One Million Words, LLC

Cover design by Mary Christopherson (mary.design)

Author photograph by Jaime Lynn Hunt (jaimelynnhunt.com)

This collection is dedicated to my mother, who taught me to embrace the weird.

Foreword

An angel, an android, and an alien walk into a book…

It's no joke. You hold in your hands a slew of short stories that span the gamut of speculative fiction, including fantasy, sci-fi, dreampunk, and paranormal.

From ambitious aliens and refined rebels to aspiring spies and darkweb denizens, all of these stories have a couple of things in common:

1. Every story suggests—or outright spotlights—the supernatural.

2. No matter what world you land in, separating the heroes from the villains won't be easy.

I suppose there's a third commonality as well: my overactive imagination spawned them all. A few tales tie into larger works—including *The Renegade Chronicles* and *The Soul Sleep Cycle*—while others are glimpses into new realms. All of them stand on their own.

But who knows? Some of these colorful characters might warrant a second look. After all, every ending opens the door to a new beginning.

—Your Author

Contents

Ghost Mode

Quentin E. Donovan—*the* Quentin E. Donovan—side-stepped into an alley, closed his eyes, and did something he hadn't done in nearly a decade.

With a deliberate twitch of his left thumb, the twin IRIS mods went offline. A whispered password triggered the auto-transcript program fueling a half-dozen feeds to quit, killing a headline about the latest darknet virus mid-scroll. Finally, he removed the sleek, pearlescent PAM—an eighth-generation iCoin Pro—from his pocket and thumbed the command to repel all incoming v-captures.

No feeds, no casts, no signals whatsoever. He was completely grid-locked.

Without the translucent menus and rolling text in his periphery, the world seemed impossibly plain. And slightly pink. It took him a moment to realize his eyes were compensating for the absence of the green tinge that always coated the corners of his vision—a much-missed reassurance that the ocular implants were successfully uploading his sensory data to the Sphere.

He shivered, as though losing his connection to the local hotspots had reduced his actual body temperature. Real-life silence usurped the subtle, soothing soundtrack of white noise in his ears.

No wonder why they call it ghost mode, he thought

morosely. The air even *tasted* dead.

Quentin returned to the main thoroughfare, where a woman was approaching from the opposite direction. He smiled politely—no, eagerly—but she didn't acknowledge him as she passed, her shaky, far-off stare skimming a number of feeds he couldn't see. For several heart-pounding seconds, he could only stand there, until he finally identified the long-forgotten feeling as solitude.

He thrust one hand inside his pocket, pressed his palm against the smooth surface of the iCoin, and flirted with the idea of rebooting all of his AR apps—longing to hear the comforting chime of the PAM booting up. But he found courage, then, in the thought of what glory lay ahead.

A pity his millions of fans wouldn't be able to enjoy the thrill of the clandestine meeting he had arranged mere hours ago on the darknet!

Releasing his hold on the hibernating PAM to rub his eyes—though that did nothing to restore the reassuring green glow of the IRIS implants—Quentin trudged the remaining block to the agreed-upon FaceCafé and entered. Without the aid of any tech, he scanned the restaurant for someone who looked out of place.

Closest to the entrance, a middle-aged woman wearing a strappy, alligator-skin dress fished a cord out of her purse and connected one end to the table's charge-port and the other to an oversized, blaze-orange PAM. The infant in the highchair beside her wailed until the woman returned the device to his or her eager little hands.

Elsewhere in the dining room, a guy in a red power suit talked to an invisible partner across the table, laughing suggestively as he adjusted his crotch.

A few tables away, a woman wearing all white swiped the air furiously with her fingers and frowned at what

Quentin could only assume was bad news. Maybe a relative had contracted that new, nasty virus the newsfeeds had been squawking about? Her smooth scalp and sheer outfit, while undoubtedly vibrant if viewed through an AR interface, looked dull and dumb in RL.

He sighed. No one appeared to be doing anything unusual.

Disappointed, he sat down at an empty table and keyed in an order for a black, half-stim coffee. He would just have to trust that the darknet lurker he had pinged—the professional villain he had promised to pay half a million Cs—would recognize him.

No worries there. He was *the* Quentin E. Donovan, after all.

The ten minutes he spent waiting, bereft of feeds and all other digital augmentation, were perfectly intolerable.

For one thing, the FaceCafé resembled a tomb. The smooth gray panels that normally flashed a parade of high-production promos, including a holotrailer for his own QED Feed, formed a bleak perimeter around the sparsely populated tables. Whatever tunes the restaurant subtly pumped into visitors' inputs couldn't reach Quentin's ears. The only sounds interrupting the sepulcher stillness were monosyllabic murmurs from the other customers and an occasional chime of the infant's PAM.

For another thing, the coffee tasted funny. He spent a full sixty seconds trying to determine if the FaceCafé's signature drink was just plain terrible or if he had never before taken the time to consider the flavor of coffee in the first place.

Pushing the acrid brew to the middle of the table, he watched the other patrons go about their wonderfully linked lives. This amused him for a while. It felt deliciously bold to stare. But after several minutes, it was obvious that he—like a real ghost—was invisible to them. Inconsequential. And observing them was akin to accessing a glitching vid that showed only half of the story.

Elbows propped on the table, he cradled his head and rubbed his temples. All of this unfiltered RL was giving him a migraine.

"Mr. Donovan?"

At last!

Looking up, he discovered two things at once: the pink haze that had haunted his peripheral vision was completely gone, and the young woman now seated across from him was a reasonably attractive specimen, even without his IRIS mods accessing her AR enhancements.

Regardless, he couldn't hide his disappointment. This was no villain.

"Yes...and who are...? Ah, but you must be a fan." He straightened his back and reclaimed the hated cup of coffee, his only prop. "You're probably wondering what happened to the QED Feed. Don't worry...we're just experiencing some technical difficulties."

The slight smile of Beautiful Stranger was unexpected. Usually, his female fans—and a significant percentage of his male demographic—downright swooned when they recognized him in public. Not that that was often. A custom-made app on his PAM permanently masked his Sphere ID to unauthorized passersby, ensuring his 24/7/365 lifecast wasn't polluted with random encounters of star-struck rubes. And by the time devotees ID'd themselves as unintended extras in any given scene, he was already en route to the next set.

But this woman's bright blue eyes weren't sending signals of excitement—sexual or otherwise. No, she looked...self-satisfied, maybe even sly...

"You're not the only one with tech issues," she said.

A few tables away, the woman in white frantically wiggled her fingers, trying to reestablish a connection to the Sphere. Meanwhile, across the room, the mom barked a few words that were banned on all but the grittiest of lifecasts while her baby tossed its unresponsive PAM to the floor. Quentin then watched the only other man there stand up and abruptly exit the FaceCafé, his obvious erection leading the way.

Turning back to Mysterious Stranger, he said, "So *that* is how you recognized me. You've lost your Sphere link too and are seeing the world through naked eyes."

She leaned back and crossed her arms, accentuating a pair of modest-sized breasts augmented neither by AR code nor cosmetic bioware. Her face was pretty, albeit in a straightforward manner. A few years back, Sphere celebs paid small fortunes to manufacture faces that looked effortlessly beautiful. However, the latest trend embraced the other extreme: exaggerated features that deemphasized traditional traits and championed dehumanizing effects.

He theorized it was her brazen adoption of outdated fashion—particularly the monochromatic shirt, naturally black hair, and the pale blue eyes unlike any gemstone—that intrigued him more than anything.

Then he remembered he was seeing her RL face. Had the Sphere connection not died and had his IRISes been online, she probably would have looked as celebulicious as anyone.

"I always see the world through naked eyes," she replied, and her pink-lipped half-smile made a repeat performance.

He chuckled lewdly at the double entendre until he

realized she was speaking literally. And was that a subtle shade of lipstick—*actual* lipstick—around her mouth?

"You can't be serious," he said. "Nobody can lead a normal life without linking to the Sphere."

"That's not what I said." Eccentric Stranger leaned forward and tapped a fingernail against the lifeless screen implanted in the center of the table. "Everyone has to plug in sometimes. A gal has to eat, though I wouldn't recommend anything from this menu...especially not the coffee."

Cup halfway to his lips, Quentin returned the foul beverage to the table.

"I said I always see *the world* through naked eyes," she continued. "When I need to make a purchase in person, I use a C-card instead of direct linking. And when I need to drop by the Sphere, I use an ancient base-model screen that takes five minutes to bloody boot up."

He scoffed. "What are you, some kind of technophobe? Or one of those zealots from the Church of Minimalists?"

She laughed, somehow sounding girly and worldly at the same time. There was no denying the woman was peculiar. She might even make an intriguing love interest during his next ratings lull. He made a mental note to file away her facepic but then remembered he was still in ghost mode.

"Actually, I've got quite a knack for tech," she replied. "This didn't happen by accident."

She punctuated her point with another tap of her fingernail against the table's blank screen. Quentin's heart pumped harder.

"*You* did this?" he asked, gesturing at the empty tables around them. "How?"

Dangerous Stranger reached beneath the conservative

neckline of her shirt and withdrew a pendant. Its white stone was a stark contrast to her black shirt. "It's a jinx charm. I scrambled Sphere links for a two-kil radius ...maybe more."

He tried to summon everything he knew about anti-Sphere terrorists and blackhats in general, but his only experiences with the Sphere's seedy underbelly was the time a jacker had blasted through all nine walls of his fire-fortress and wreaked havoc while impersonating him— *the* Quentin E. Donovan—on the Sphere.

The jacker, who turned out to be only a grayhat, hadn't siphoned any money or done any significant damage during what turned out to be a foolish prank. On the contrary, the QED Feed had enjoyed a huge ratings spike.

His fingers twitched, eager to reactivate his PAM and do a search for "jinx charm" and "citiZEN"—the Sphere's most notorious anarchists—or better yet, power up his IRISes and upload that pretty little face of hers to CrimeCheck. But considering the table's screen wasn't even displaying an apologetic out-of-order alert, the woman's pendant had done more than just disrupt Sphere connectivity.

She had somehow crippled tech itself.

A single thought surfaced above his mounting panic: aside from that grayhat prankster, he had encountered *one* other denizen of the darknet...

"You! You're the...the..."

Devious Villain chuckled. "Wow, that took you long enough to piece together. I guess fans of the QED Feed aren't tuning in for mental stimulation."

"But why...why did you...?" An eloquent ad libber—unlike Donna Rom, whose entire lifecast was irrefutably scripted—Quentin was unaccustomed to speechlessness. He took a sip of terrible, cold coffee to buy some time.

She tucked the pendant beneath her shirt and crossed her arms. "I thought you'd appreciate some privacy while we discussed our transaction. Defending against eavesdroppers in the d-net can take an hour of prep, but knock out everybody's tech in the real world, and you'll always clear the room."

Her crooked smile stretched wider. "And what better way to make sure I'm not the next guest star on your little lifecast?"

"I told you I would be in ghost mode," he snapped, hoping irritation would mask the full measure of his fear.

"I don't typically take people at their word, chief."

"Yes...well..." He took a deep, steadying breath. Despite the anxiety gnawing at his not-too-slight-but-not-too-round gut, a part of him relished the repartee. If only he had some way to record it! He might even consider taking a page out of Donna Rom's playbook and reconstruct the scene under more ideal circumstances—editing out his stammers and casting a more cam-friendly vixen to play the part of Villain.

She crossed her arms and smirked. "Let me see if I have this right. You ventured into the d-net because you were desperate for some excitement. Your show has what...six months?...a year tops?...before people realize there's nothing more to know about you. And even if a few diehard fans continue to follow your feed, your time among the Top Trending is just about over. You need...how did you put it?...'a dramatic encounter with a true villain' to spice things up."

"Yes," he answered, and his voice cracked mortifyingly. "But I don't want it all scripted out. The element of surprise is essential for theatrical spontaneity. I'm not even sure why we're having this *pre*-meeting. I—"

She planted her palms on the tabletop and leaned

forward suddenly. The pose reminded him of any number of jungle hunters from the Nat Geo feed. "We're *here* because even though we're going to do this thing my way, I'm letting you have some input. But that can change, Quentin F. Donovan."

He swallowed a large lump of something that tasted of bad coffee and brass.

She laughed, and her predatory posture reverted to an easy recline. "Yeah, I know you changed your name from Quentin Francis Donovan to Quentin Emerson Donovan a few weeks before your show started. I'm betting you did it so that your lifecast could be called QED, not out of appreciation for a certain transcendentalist writer's work."

Truth be told, Quentin knew nothing about Ralph Waldo Emerson, other than his name sounded both literary and dignified. The woman was also correct in assuming he had wanted his lifecast to harken back to the Latin *quod erat demonstrandum* in support of his branding as an intellectual. It wasn't a pun exactly, but he had found some amusement in giving his lifecast a name that essentially translated to "What Was to be Shown."

Yet he saw no reason to confirm her suspicions, so he said nothing.

This was her show.

"What exactly did you have in mind when you sent a single-target query into the d-net?" she asked. "How far are you willing to go for your...um...'art'?"

If he had been sitting across from anyone else, he would have pointed out that living life to the fullest for the benefit of millions of viewers *was* an art. But even as his breakfast settled back down into its appropriate anatomical position, he realized how absurd it was to expect the villain and the hero to see eye to eye.

He cleared his throat. "As you may or may not know, violence is starting to trend again Sphere-wide. Apparently, enough time has passed since the last large-scale tragedy. However, with the latest CrimeCheck upgrades, even the slowest-witted thugs understand there's almost nowhere on the planet one can attack another human being without being seen. I visited the darknet to find someone who might have a means of scrambling the authorities' inputs...*without* knocking out the QED Feed.

"What I had in mind was a random assault...something that would provide a few strategically placed bruises, maybe require some stitches, and result in a night or two in the hospital."

He would be able to spin the incident any number of ways, though he wasn't sure which angle would get the most play. A random act of violence would be the most shocking initially, but that narrative had a relatively short shelf life. Concocting a storyline about a disgruntled fan, on the other hand, seemed too obvious. He might have considered framing his rival for hiring the villain, except the publicity would benefit Donna Rom as much as him.

"So you want me to kick your ass?" she asked.

"Quaintly put," he replied, feeling much more in character now. "Yes, that was what I had in mind initially, but given the circumstances and the...*dynamics* of our particular dyad, I'm no longer certain that scenario is ideal."

She rolled her eyes. "Are you trying to tell me you have cold feet?"

"No, not per se. What I mean is the pain itself is not a deterrent, but rather the...well...delivery system."

She stared at him blankly.

"After meeting you today...and *seeing* you...I am concerned that, given the differences in our gender, well..."

His throat suddenly drier than Donna Rom's latest

storyline, he reached for the evil coffee. Its cool temperature had nothing on the villain's icy look.

"You don't want to get beaten up by a woman."

He raised his hands reassuringly—and defensively. "What I meant to say is, given your demographic, which includes not only your gender, but also your age, race, and build, I'm just not sure how *believable* it would be for your character to attack mine."

"Oh, I promise my urge to punch you in the face right now is *very* believable." Her half-smile made him flinch. "But that would be a waste, wouldn't it? No cameras recording. No adoring fans to sob as the blood gushes from your perfectly sculpted nose."

He wiped the sweat from his forehead. "Yes...well... please don't take it personally when I tell you that I would like to explore other talent—"

"How far are you willing to go for your art?"

"I...I'm happy to pay you a stipend for your time today. Which account should I—"

She leaned forward again. "Would you die for it?"

Her words stole the breath from his body as effectively as the jinx charm had sucked the Sphere signals from the room. Instinct commanded him to run, but he couldn't remember the last time he moved faster than a brisk walk. Besides, the woman looked like she probably sprinted just for sport.

"I have a lot of money. Name your price to walk away."

She shifted back in her seat, but her nonchalant pose did nothing to dispel the apprehension that python-squeezed his chest. "I know exactly how many Cs you have stashed away, including your crypted accounts. I've already helped myself to a healthy advance."

"I'll pay you twice as much to leave me in peace!"

"Where's the fun in that?" she asked without a trace of mirth in her voice. "You chose to play a dangerous game, and we're going to see it through. You have two options. Either I kill you here and now without a soul to witness it and without any footage to preserve your life's tragic climax or..."

He leaned forward in spite of himself.

"...you kill Quentin E. Donovan."

"S-suicide?"

She shrugged. "In a manner of speaking. I can delete all traces of the QED Feed in a matter of minutes, but you have to cut the cord on this Sphere-centric half-life of yours and make ghost mode your default setting. Quentin E. Donovan dies today, either physically or figuratively."

The FaceCafé spun around him. He fought for air. Searching for signs of madness in her eyes, he implored any of the long-defunct deities to reveal this to be a distasteful joke.

But her stern expression didn't waver, and he could only assume her soul was as black as the metaphorical hat she wore.

"Please—"

"Try to bribe me again, and I'll kill you right now."

"Oh God..."

His tears flowed freely. Wiping a pristine sleeve under his nose, he forced himself to take a series of even breaths. He had a decision to make, and while part of him was eager to make any vow that would stave off bodily harm, another voice fought for the preservation of something far greater than this mortal coil.

Which scenario ensured his legacy would live on after the QED Feed's demise: the discovery of his murdered body in a random FaceCafé or the mystery borne of his sudden disappearance from the Sphere?

"But what...what would I do without my show? Who would I be?" he asked, posing the question as much to himself as to the deadly antagonist.

"Someone real," she replied.

"Why are you doing this to me?"

She smirked again. "If you have to ask the question, you won't understand the answer. Anyway, you should be thanking me. Not many d-netters are as sporting as I am. Now make your choice, or I'll make it for you."

She withdrew a silver handgun from under the table. Like her pink lipstick, the pistol was a relic from another age, a prop from some retro whodunit vid. The barrel pointed not at his chest, but at his head.

Getting gunned down by the anachronistic femme fatale would have made an amazing ending to the QED Feed. However, there was no way for this story to be told. And getting blasted full in the face would also rob him of an open casket, reducing the cross-feed coverage significantly.

Live in obscurity or die in obscurity—which was worse?

She cocked the gun, a gesture that always seemed ridiculous in the classic vids but, in person, was powerful enough to liberate the contents of his bladder.

"OK, OK, I don't want to die! I'll go off the grid...hell, I'll even join the Church of Minimalists if you'll just leave me alone!"

She lowered her gun. "And trade one cult for another? No, my terms are pretty simple...but not painless, I'm afraid. The first thing we have to do is get rid of all that tech inside your head."

She reached under the neckline of her blouse, and he expected the jinx charm to make a reprise. But she by-passed the pendant and retrieved something farther down, an object that must have been wedged between breast and brassiere. It was a trope as old-fashioned as the undergarment itself.

Villain sprang forward and plunged something sharp into the back of his hand. He recoiled, spilling the forgotten coffee. The dark liquid washed over the side of the table and pooled, blood-like, on the floor below.

"What the hell did—?" Pain exploded from the core of his brain, obliterating the rest of his words.

In between his own screams, he heard her say, "Don't worry...blindness...temporary..."

Then the woman, the FaceCafé, and the rest the world melted beneath a searing white light.

He awoke with a groan in his sparse, one-room house and knew he had been dreaming of his old life again.

While details of the subconscious-driven storyline were sparse, he knew he had been happy, *alive*! But now the trite soundtrack of birdsong beckoned him back to his eternal gig in ghost mode. In contrast to the stimulating imagery of those fast-fading scenes, the wooden planks of his ceiling looked unbearably boring.

He sighed and closed his eyes. While the residents of the peaceful, grid-locked community treated him well enough, quitting tech cold turkey had proven a tumultuous transition. He could never have attempted it out there in the civilized world. Fortunately, the remote settlement—most people just called it Ghost Town—was bereft of temptation.

Well, *mostly* bereft, he thought.

Slowly, surreptitiously, he pulled the dormant iCoin Pro from his sweat-stained pillowcase.

Dreams about his old life never failed to arouse a deep

desire to renege on his promise to the villain, consequences be damned. And while he had always managed to resist the Sphere's siren call so far, time had dulled his fear.

In fact, on some of the most tedious days—when his neighbor prattled on about the recent rain's impact on her tomato plants or he couldn't force his eyes to read one more page of so-called literature—he almost craved a second confrontation with Supposed Savior.

Anything to inject some stimulation into the emptiness of RL.

He didn't know how long he lay there, running his fingers along the ridged rim of the contraband machine, fantasizing about booting up. Was Donna Rom still in the Top Trending? What would his fans say if the QED Feed had a new update after nearly a year of silence?

His pulse raced as he wondered what harm a short "I'm still alive!" post could do.

It's not as if the deadly doomsday virus his neighbors constantly whispered about could hurt him, not unless he found a way to replace his IRISes and the rest of the implants she had destroyed.

His thumb caressed the tiny power button on the edge of the PAM. With each pass, he played with the pressure, nudging it a little harder each time. His breathing quickened as he envisioned the many feeds he yearned to visit—albeit it on the PAM's tiny screen.

He was so caught up in his reverie that he initially mistook the excited voices on the other side of his crooked wooden door as competing audio feeds. But when his spoken command to mute the PAM went ignored, the truth struck him like a slap across the face.

An actual crowd had gathered in the typically tranquil town square.

He stumbled out of the creaky bed, hobbled by a

combination of poor circulation and mounting panic. Nothing exciting ever happened in Ghost Town, and the outside world—the *connected* world—seldom intruded. He wondered what news could have caused such a commotion.

A knock at the door made him squeeze the PAM guiltily.

"Wake up!" shouted a voice from outside. "It actually happened! The e-plague mutated. Now even folks without mods are contracting it. Anyone who accesses the Sphere risks getting infected...anyone! Can you hear me, Francis? Francis?"

The *former* Quentin E. Donovan didn't answer. He could only stare in horror at the blue-green glow of the PAM's power light leaking through his clenched fingers. Then the silence was broken by the cheerful chime of his secondhand iCoin Pro.

Anthropology in Apogee

A surge of excitement and anxiety electrifies my skin as I consider what is on the other side of the door.

The nanites in my bloodstream compensate, returning my heartbeats to their regular rhythm. I take a deep breath, not because an increase in oxygen or carbon dioxide or nitrogen will aid my biology in any way, but because the gesture is a familiar one to our greeters. I remind myself to smile, and since I have practiced this primal expression for months, the muscles that ring my mouth ache only a little.

Beside me, Tuu mimics my grin. The ambassador has forgotten to relax his eyes though, so it could be mistaken for a grimace. At least Tuu is trying. Ysa, on the other hand—and on the other side of Tuu—does not even attempt a smile. I wish again that Ysa had not been included in the delegation, not for such an important occasion. However, I cannot argue that the xenobiologist is the most qualified in her field.

And after all, it was I who had reminded Tuu that the number three holds significance with the humans.

When the door starts to flicker, indicating its inevitable fluctuation from a solid state to stationary electrons and space, I face forward, eager to catch a glimpse of the species I have studied for so long. I take another deep breath.

The sheer number of them astounds me, though we all knew our arrival would attract a lot of attention. We are the first of our kind to physically visit their world, the first of any extraplanetary beings to walk upon Earth.

As we glide down to where their envoys await us, I regret not insisting more strongly for stairs or a ramp. The key to our acceptance is emphasizing our similarities, not our superiority. Although the majority of those receiving us—the ones carrying signs that say, "Welcome to Earth," and, "We Love Seraphs"—smile and cheer, our reconnaissance suggests many humans do not see us or our wings as angel-like at all.

Unsurprisingly, those who vocally oppose our presence in this solar system have not been invited to the ceremony.

The human ambassador extends his hand in greeting, and Tuu accepts it. I am sure he does not recall the significance of the gesture, let alone its medieval origin, but I am pleased he remembers to squeeze only as hard as his counterpart. Touch is important to the humans, despite their frail anatomy.

I know I should be paying more attention to the alien delegates as introductions are made, but I cannot help but lose myself in the spectacle. I have studied humans for so long—ever since our probe first picked up their signals from this otherwise-empty plot of space—and the cheering crowd around me is so much more vibrant, more *alive* than the video feeds and the virtual interactions I have experienced.

So many different sizes, colors, and sounds!

I force myself to focus when the human ambassador indicates a man to his right, Earth's finest astrobiologist. I refresh my smile, squinting my eyes in genuine happiness, for it is indeed a pleasure to finally meet Dr. Brahm-bhatt face to face. Even though he is average height for a human male, he seems so much shorter in person. I bend over ever so slightly to shake his hand, which is very warm.

Forgetting my scripted greeting, I tell him, "I apologize if my skin feels uncomfortably cold. We can alter our metabolism if you think it will put your people more at ease."

He waves away the suggestion, an act that causes Ysa's ears to swell in confusion. "No one you meet today will be bothered by such things," Dr. Brahmbhatt says.

What he does not say is that our detractors—those humans who call us space demons instead of seraphs—have already spread the word through their global media that we are cold-blooded creatures. Ysa had rankled at the rumor because it is biologically untrue. However, I am more disturbed by the cultural implication that we are an uncaring species comparable to Earth's reptiles.

During the hour of pageantry that follows, I remember to shift my weight occasionally, though neither my musculature nor my circulation requires it. I also scratch nonexistent itches on my arms.

Ysa does not follow suit, standing as unsettlingly still as a statue while Tuu shares how deeply touched he is by Earth's warm welcome. The ambassador's inflections are appropriately modulated. He surely sounds as sincere to the humans as he feels, which took a fair amount of coaching from myself.

The expressions of the onlookers support my hypothesis. Every human is smiling, except for those whose visages' are wrinkled in concentration as they record Tuu's speech with bulky cameras on three legs. I remind myself that we are making *history*, and yet it takes additional intercession from my nanites to calm me when I see the soldiers standing guard near our vessel. Their weapons shoot small pieces of metal, an apparatus not much more sophisticated than what their rock-throwing ancestors used but just as brutal and deadly.

I reflect that Earth's history is rife with catastrophe and violence.

When Dr. Brahmbhatt offers his arm to escort me down from the dais, I happily accept. I am eager to trade the crowd, well-meaning though it is, for a more personal environment and make a mental note to write a paper about the possible effects of agoraphobia on future envoys to Earth.

There are simply so many humans packed together on this planet!

Walking beside Dr. Brahmbhatt, I try to identify his smells without noticeably dilating my olfactory slits. He is wearing an artificial scent—cologne, I suspect—but beneath that I can detect a musk reminiscent of animals reserved for high feasts back home. My sudden flare in appetite fills me with shame. I wonder what I smell like to him but decide not to ask, knowing humans tend to be self-conscious of how they are perceived as well as how they perceive others.

For some reason I have not yet discovered, they equate courtesy with censorship of their feelings.

"I think that went well," Dr. Brahmbhatt says, his mustache moving a little above his smile. I want to touch it to gauge whether the hair is soft or bristly. But I do not.

I make a point to nod as I reply. "Yes, I look forward to sharing your broadcasts with our people."

I do not tell Dr. Brahmbhatt that most of my kind will

not bother to watch it. While a first visit to a new popu-lated planet does not happen every day—or even every year—the fanfare itself hardly sparks excitement among my kind. The initial curiosity about the short, compact, patchy-furred species called humanity has long since worn off for many.

As much as I want to observe Dr. Brahmbhatt further, I spare a moment to study Tuu, who walks beside the President of the United Nations, the closest rank Earth has to a planetary leader. Tuu's posture is very stiff compared to the President's, but at least my colleague remembers to swing his arms a little as he matches the slow pace of his escort.

A glance back at Ysa reveals the xenobiologist is making no efforts to alter her precise, measured move-ments. Ysa answers the questions of her escort—a sup-posed expert in our own physiology—with clipped responses and without looking at the man.

No, I correct myself, she is a woman.

I let my tongue ripple in satisfaction, privately thankful when we leave the last traces of the crowd behind. We approach three long, wheeled vehicles, which will take us away from the public celebration to the true purpose of our visit: a secluded discussion about the shared future of our peoples.

Tuu's ears puff up a little. "The agenda you submitted and which we approved detailed a single transport to our destination."

The President of the United Nations smiles—nerv-ously? reassuringly?—and says, "After further considera-tion for your safety, we decided against putting all of our distinguished guests in one limousine."

I think of an Earth idiom—something about eggs or Easter baskets—but cannot bring the saying fully to mind.

Beside me, Ysa says, "Quantity over quality…this is Earth after all."

I hope no one heard her or, at least, was able to translate her swift, softly spoken words. At Dr. Brahmbhatt's insistence, I join him in the second vehicle, which, to my surprise, is capacious enough for me to sit fully upright and stretch out my legs. Dr. Brahmbhatt takes a seat across from me and continues to smile.

I echo his expression, even though the muscles around my mouth have begun to protest a little.

"You can stop smiling now," Dr. Brahmbhatt tells me.

I relax my lips into what a human would call a slight frown. "I did not wish to appear aloof, Dr. Brahmbhatt."

"The cameras are off, and I can read your body language just fine."

"Oh really?" I ask, emphasizing the tonal rise in the last syllable. I hope it sounds playful.

He leans forward, elbows on his knees. "Absolutely. Your shoulders are raised, indicating you are relaxed, and the slight vibrations of your lips tells me you are not trying to hide the undulations of your tongue. You are indeed happy to be here."

"As are you, Dr. Brahmbhatt…unless your increased heartrate is due to fear and not, as I suspect, delight."

Dr. Brahmbhatt laughed. "Don't tell my family, but this is irrefutably the best day of my life. And please, call me Parth. We are friends, are we not?"

A month ago, I might have argued, but I have since spent a significant amount of time researching human names—given names, surnames, even nicknames—and I now understand the significance of downgrading from a respectful, professional designation to a more intimate variation.

"Very well, Parth. Please call me Miranda."

His bushy black eyebrows rise. "A human name? I assure you that is not necessary—"

"Please," I repeat. "It will make it easier during my stay here on Earth."

Dr. Brahmbhatt nods. "As will choosing a pronoun, I imagine, though the media has been pretty good about using 'they' in both singular and plural to refer to your people."

Recalling some of the jokes in our ongoing corre-spondence, I say, "Yes, you humans are so very particular about gender as well as preoccupied with sex. I have heard our mono-gendered species has inspired many porno-graphic productions here on Earth."

Dr. Brahmbhatt's color alters suddenly, his brown cheeks acquiring a reddish tint. Anger? No, I realize. Embarrassment. Even though sexuality holds prominence in many aspects of human life, I remember too late that acknowledging that fact is taboo.

He clears his throat. "Yes, well, your lack of gender distinction also contributed to the mainstream comparison of your people with angels."

"And demons," I add.

Dr. Brahmbhatt sighs. "Yes, well, we can't seem to get along with ourselves much of the time. Introducing 'out-siders' just gives the unenlightened another target for their intolerance and…wait, why are we stopping?"

Forehead wrinkled with worry, Dr. Brahmbhatt turns and knocks on a dark pane of glass behind him. "Is every-thing—?"

Before he can finish his question, the interior window opens, and a hand stretches through. There a small flash, a deafening blast. Dr. Brahmbhatt's limp body falls forward onto my lap.

*　　　*　　　*

I have witnessed humanity's brutal nature from afar. Those two-dimensional examples of violence—both captured from reality and recreated in their fiction—are always alarming and have proven impossible to acclimate myself to.

Seeing the hole in Dr. Brahmbhatt's head and feeling his hot blood spattered against my face and dripping down my legs paralyzes me. My mind cannot make sense of what has transpired. I am absently aware of the nanites increasing circulation to my brain and a blast of adrenaline through my limbs, kickstarting survival instincts rendered nearly extinct centuries ago.

I try to remember my training. Self-defense lessons are an essential curriculum for anyone visiting an inhabited world. But all I can do is stare down in sadness at the corpse of my only friend on Earth. Without quite knowing why, I say, "Rest in peace, Parth."

A harsh laugh from the other side of the small window —from the driver—usurps my attention. "Rest in peace? More like rot in *hell*, traitor!"

I cannot see the one who speaks, but the low voice suggests a human male. I catch only a fraction of his face in a small hanging mirror as I gently slide Dr. Brahmbhatt to the vehicle's floor. The driver's skin is a light hue. His eyes are hidden behind lenses, also mirrors.

My nanites have quelled the panic within me, but that does not stop me from lowering my shoulders anxiously. I try to remember what I learned of self-defense combat. It had been all so academic, so abstract. Strange choreography rehearsed for a performance that should never come.

With the metallic scent of Dr. Brahmbhatt's blood

filling my olfactory slits, I know that the chlorine-rich vapors of my own body fluids will soon mingle with the stench.

Ears swollen to maximum size, I wait for the hand to reappear, for the ugly black mechanism to emerge and shoot its tiny mineral into my flesh. It is possible the nanites will be able to mitigate the damage of the wound and stabilize me, depending on where the bullet hits. It is possible I might survive this, though not likely.

Not if the man shoots me in the head too.

Yet there is no movement in the window. My arms stretch out in alarm when the door I had entered earlier opens suddenly. I see the gun first. The river of regret that floods through my thoughts cascades into a singular, unifying sorrow: my death will destroy all hope of a peaceful coexistence with the humans.

Anthropology as a study as well as all attempts to preserve this fascinating species will end abruptly.

"Come on out, *Miranda*," says the driver with a sneer. There can be no mistaking the lopsided grin for anything other than a spiteful expression.

As I obey, I cling to the hope that I can somehow talk my way out of this. Human psychology is impressively complex but also frustratingly inconsistent. The next few words out of my mouth might prevent an intergalactic conflict or ignite one.

So I say nothing as I place a hand on either side of the doorframe and pull myself outside. Something—possibly the nanites—reminds me I could fly up and away from danger, making the man's shot more difficult or, at least, nonlethal. However, I keep my feet planted firmly on the ground. I clasp my hands in front of me, an unnatural stance for my kind, but one that should convey calm or even humility.

I see myself reflected in his glasses. I am not smiling. I consider frowning or widening my eyes but think better of it. Our eyes are already perceived as unnervingly large for some humans. And I have never mastered the ability to tremble.

"Look…at…*you*," the man says. "Like something out of a monster movie."

I cock my head to one side, trying to look interested in what he has to say and keeping my gaze away from the hard hunk of death in his hand.

"I am not a monster," I say softly, soothingly. "I am a—"

"Seraph?" he asks with another sneer. "There's nothing holy, nothing *godly* about you. And I hate to be the one to tell you, but Earth First isn't going to let you take our planet."

"We are here to *help* Earth."

The wicked laugh echoes through the empty canyon. I do not know how the man was able to separate our vehicle from the caravan and navigate to this remote location. Conspiracy, most likely. This driver is not the only human possessed by hate and fear.

"That's what you aliens are always saying…how you're going to be our saviors…feed the hungry, heal the sick, refreeze the icecaps or whatever," the man says. "But I don't buy it. What you're offering is too good to be true. Anyway, we never asked for your help."

"Some of you did," I reply.

I regret my counterpoint when he takes two powerful steps forward. "Traitors! If we let a bunch of outsiders interfere, using technology and 'evolved reasoning' to fix everything, then we won't be human anymore…won't be in control of our own destiny. No, this is *our* planet, and *we're* gonna be the ones who save it."

My studies suggest I should keep him talking. Empathy might prevent further loss of life. I know I really ought to agree with him.

"What if you cannot save it?" I ask.

The man's voice gets quiet. "Then we deal with it ourselves. We face the consequences without a bunch of blue-skinned, bird-winged, bug-eyed overlords looking over our shoulders."

I glance back at the vehicle, at Dr. Brahmbhatt's lifeless body. "Even if it means more death?"

He snorts. "For all your advancements, you *angels* can't seem to get it through your big brains that you can't force people to something they're not…to be 'good'… and that when you do, it just makes us fight back."

"You have not yet tried our way," I say.

"And *you* obviously haven't studied our history enough. If you try to 'liberate' us against our will, you're gonna have a bona fide Vietnam on your hands."

I cannot make sense of that last part. But while I do not know everything about humanity's past, I do know about my own people—our history and our governing philosophy.

"If you kill me, it will only make things worse for Earth."

He raises his gun up to my face. "Are you threatening me, Miranda?"

"No, I am warning you."

"Noted," he says through his teeth. "Unfortunately for you, Earth First needs a win, a show of strength…and that means you have to die."

To my surprise, I am no longer afraid. The sadness filling me is not for my own demise or even what my death will mean for Earth's future, but for the man holding the gun. His pain is palpable. I can smell his fear.

"I forgive you," I tell him.

"I don't care."

The second crack of gunfire reverberates through the canyon. No light flashes from the barrel of the driver's gun. Instead, the blast erupts from the back of the weapon, which falls from the man's fingers just as his neck explodes in a spray of bright red blood.

He falls face-first into the dust, smashing his glasses into two pieces.

Later, I will learn how the gun miraculously misfired, but that will not be until after the helicopters and squadron of soldiers in open-air vehicles swoop in to take me some-where safe. For the next several minutes, all I can do is stare at myself in that cracked mirror lens—the broken glasses of a broken man from a broken world.

I form my lips into a smile as I vow to do everything I can to help humanity—whether it is wanted or not.

Gamechanger

FEINT

a movement made to deceive an adversary; often an attack aimed at one place merely to serve as a distraction from the actual intended target or point of attack.

(In other words, a trick.)

Asher closed the cover of the *Monstrous Manual* at the sound of tires on gravel.

She actually came! he thought with a smile.

"She actually came," Lorenzo muttered from the swiveling chair beside him.

Ignoring the disappointment in his best friend's voice, Asher tossed the battered book onto his bed and dashed into the hallway—though not fast enough to miss another almost-under-his-breath remark from Lorenzo.

"I still don't know why you invited *her*."

Over his shoulder, Asher yelled, "The more, the merrier!"

He might have added that Mezzo-Earth had plenty of room for more players. Or he could have mentioned that every good company of heroes—from the Fellowship of the Ring to the Companions of the Hall—benefited from a diversity of skills and abilities.

Besides, he thought as he sock-slid across the hard-wood floor, two adventurers were partners at best. But *three*? Three was the beginning of an actual party!

Asher's enthusiasm hiccupped as he opened the door and saw the girl astride her bike in the driveway. With her grinning-skull T-shirt and ripped jeans, Makayla Schmidt didn't look like the type who'd geek out on games, let alone what Asher had planned that afternoon.

But she had come. There was hope.

"Hey, Mak." He nodded at her hockey stick. "Did you come right from practice?"

Mak dismounted, letting her bike crash to the ground. Reversing her grip on the hockey stick and holding it up so it looked more like a sickle than a sporting gear, she chuckled. "Practice starts at the ass crack of dawn. I've been home for hours. I just brought my stick in case I ran into any douchebags on the shortcut through the woods."

Asher winced, praying his mom was out of earshot of what she called "coarse language."

"Well, you might as well bring it inside with you," he said. "Depending on which weapon you choose, it could make a good prop. Think of it as Plan A."

"I thought you said this was an outside game," Mak replied, following him into the house.

"It is, but you need to create your character before we can start."

When they reached his bedroom, Asher closed the door behind them, putting a couple inches of wood between his parents and Mak's conversational cussing. Then he waited for his two guests to acknowledge each other's existence.

Lorenzo didn't look up from the *Dragonlance* book he had pulled off Asher's shelf earlier that morning. Mak set her hockey stick against his headboard, looked around the room, and said, "Wow."

It was the first time a friend other than Lorenzo had entered his inner sanctum of nerdiness. Suddenly self-conscious of the dragon poster, hand-drawn maps of Mezzo-Earth on his desk, and row upon row of fantasy novels lining the walls, he looked to his best friend since second grade for support.

Lorenzo Lopez turned the page and kept reading.

Unable to decide whether to sit on the bed or stay standing, Asher adopted an awkward position halfway between the two, his leg bent painfully beneath him. "So, Mak, how much do you know about larping?"

Mak leaned against his dresser. "Just what you guys told me on the way home from school yesterday, right before you said I could try it out today if I wanted. You guys pretend to be elves and fight monsters and what-ever."

A sigh from Lorenzo.

Asher smiled patiently. "It's a little more complicated than that. I'm the gamemaster…or GM…which means I guide the story. I also play the role of Elvish Presley, an elf minstrel. Lorenzo is Sir Larpsalot, a human paragon, which is basically a paladin."

"A what?" Mak asked.

Another sigh from Lorenzo.

"A holy knight," Asher said. "Up until now, we've been the only two heroes—"

"Ooh, so I get to be the villain?" Mak asked, her eyes widening.

Lorenzo tossed his book aside. "The GM controls the enemies. If you're gonna play with us, you have to be a hero too."

"But I get to make up my own character, right?" Mak

asked. "Is this the part where we roll a bunch of weird-looking dice?"

Interrupting Lorenzo's third sigh, Asher said, "We're not that formal. In tabletop games, like Dungeons & Dragons, there are a lot of rules and restrictions. Lorenzo and I have a more casual approach. Plus its larping, so it'd be kind of hard to make attack rolls and saving throws."

Mak stared blankly at him, perhaps regretting her decision to delve into the dorky lives of her fellow seventh graders.

For the next few minutes, Asher did his best to summarize—and simplify—the world of Mezzo-Earth, which had started out as a parody of Tolkien's setting but had evolved, over the past year, into a full-fledged fantasy realm in its own right.

As he explained the types of creatures that populated Mezzo-Earth and the adventurer categories he had invented, Mak plopped down on his bed and started thumbing through the old-school bestiary.

"Then there are foresters," Asher continued. "They're a lot like rangers from D&D and tend to be good at—"

"This." Mak turned the *Monstrous Manual* toward him and pointed at the hulking form of a half-man, half-bull.

"A minotaur?" Asher asked.

"Yeah, I wanna be a minotaur."

Lorenzo laughed. "You can't be a monster."

Mak glared at him. "I can't be a bad guy. I can't be a minotaur. If you say I have to be some sad-ass fairy princess, I'm gonna kick *your*—"

"You can be minotaur," Asher quickly interjected. "They're usually fierce melee fighters, but we can explore other classifications if you want."

Looking down at the page, Mak said, "This is what I want. Big muscles, a huge axe, horns…you can't get more metal than that."

Lorenzo crossed his arms. "Sounds like your character is a real brute."

"A *berserker*," Asher corrected.

"So why would I, a paragon of virtue, and you, the noble Minstrel King, ally ourselves with a minotaur berserker?" Lorenzo asked. "Sounds kind of farfetched, even for Mezzo-Earth."

Asher was about to point out that a Knight of Solamnia became fast friends with a minotaur in the *Dragonlance* books, but then Mak jumped up from the bed to loom over Lorenzo. The boy almost fell out of his seat.

"Keep giving me attitude, Lopez, and I'll pound your character into paragon paste."

Lorenzo raised his hands in surrender. "I'm just saying our alignments probably don't…you know what? Never mind. Asher is a pro at spinning stories. I'm sure he'll make it work."

In truth, Asher's mind was already stampeding ahead with possibilities. "So what's your character's name, Mak?"

She smiled darkly. "Brutus."

"Brutus?" Lorenzo asked. "That doesn't sound like a girl's name."

"That's because Brutus isn't a girl. Is that gonna be a problem too?" Mak looked from Lorenzo to Asher.

"Not a problem," Asher replied at the same time Lorenzo said, "Nope."

Eager to escape the confines of his bedroom—which seemed too small for cold-shoulder Lorenzo and hot-headed Mak—Asher led his friends outside.

As he opened the door, a boisterous blur of red-brown

fur leaped up at Mak.

"Jabber, down! *Down!*" Asher tried to grab ahold of the dog's collar but missed. "Sorry. He just gets excited when somebody new shows up. He must've been out back when you got here."

Mak dropped to her knees and scratched behind the golden retriever's ears. Jabber licked her nose, and she laughed. "Look at this tough guy. Such a good guard dog, aren't you? Aren't you?"

Asher could only stand there, amazed and amused to see the tough girl acting so...*girly*.

Still running her fingers through Jabber's long fur, Mak asked, "Can we bring him along?"

Before Asher could answer, Lorenzo said, "No way. We've tried that before. Jabber just gets in the way and ruins the game."

Mak patted Jabber's head and looked up at Asher. He didn't want to say no to her, but Lorenzo was right. They had once cast Jabber in the role of a wily young dragon-ling—the Jabberwacky—and had spent more time trying to wrangle the excited dog than waging anything akin to a battle against him. Even the times they brought him along because Asher's parents forced them, Jabber whined nonstop, pacing back in forth by the tree they had tied his lead to.

"Sorry, Mak," Asher said. "Not this time."

Mak glared past Asher at Lorenzo. "Are you sure *you're* not the villain, Lopez?"

Lorenzo rolled his eyes. "Where do you want to do this, Asher? The camp on your property? The creek at Hobbs Woods? The corn fields?"

Hoping to regain some goodwill with the prospective party member, Asher said, "It's Mak's backstory. Why don't we let her decide?"

Mak kicked one leg over her bike and slung her hockey stick across the handlebars. "Hmm…where would a tough SOB like Brutus hang out? Wait, I got it…follow me!"

Without warning, Mak spun her bike around and sped down the driveway, back toward the country road.

Asher was still nudging back his kickstand when Lorenzo pulled up next to him. "This is a bad idea. Mark my words."

Lorenzo put on his football helmet—a stand-in for Sir Larpsalot's golden helm—and rode after Mak.

Asher hurried to catch up. "If you'd lighten up a little, you might actually have some fun today."

"I know you're excited to have another player." Not even the helmet could hide Lorenzo's frown. "Just don't get your hopes up too high. Makayla Schmidt is not like us. She's a neighbor, not a friend. I'm not even sure she *has* any friends."

"We'll see," Asher said, wrapping his homemade cape around him so it wouldn't get stuck in the spokes.

"I just don't want her to ruin our game." Lorenzo increased his speed, leaving Asher, literally, in the dust.

Stifling a cough, Asher couldn't deny that today could change the game forever. The old two-player sessions worked well enough, but Asher craved a wider cast of characters. He needed to find a way to show Lorenzo that growth was a good thing.

And to do that, Asher would have to control the narrative like never before.

Asher watched Mak skid to a stop a couple of feet from the drop-off.

"We're here!" she announced with a mischievous grin.

The boys stopped much farther back from the ledge

and exchanged uneasy looks.

"The quarry is off limits," Lorenzo stated, sounding more like his lawful-good alter ego than he probably realized.

Mak dropped her bike to the ground. Hefting her hockey stick against her shoulder, she said, "What, are you scared, Lopez?"

"Of the quarry? No. Of getting caught trespassing? Uh, *yeah*?"

Glancing across the enormous chasm, which appeared deserted this particular Saturday afternoon, Asher suspected Lorenzo was more worried about his parents finding out than being spotted by any quarry employees. That's exactly how Asher felt anyway.

Mak scoffed. "Brutus lives in the mountains. This is his territory."

Looking out at the deep hole, Asher felt both friends' stares boring into him. Today was about balance. If he was going to make this session fun for Lorenzo and Mak, he had to keep both players happy.

He cleared his throat. "As it so happens, our adventure begins in the Crooked Spine Spires, on the *summit* of the tallest mountain."

Lorenzo shook his head. Mak grinned.

Brutus the Bullheaded was stubborn, even by minotaur standards.

Some in the Steer Clear Clan attributed this to a tragedy in Brutus's youth, when, during the young minotaur's first raid, he watched his father, Beau Vine, get butchered by the brave defenders of a frontier burg. After that, Brutus's bloodlust became insatiable, as though every villager he beheaded might somehow bring back the clan's old patriarch.

"Wait, Brutus is a raider? Are you sure I'm not the villain?" Mak asked.

But as Brutus grew from a scrawny half-calf into a muscular bull-*man*, he began to question the wisdom behind sacking the same three towns over and over again. He dreamed of greater glory, a greater purpose—

"And greater challenges," Mak prompted.

—and greater challenges.

Brutus the Bullheaded often locked horns with Black Angus, the dark-furred chieftain who had stepped up after Beau Vine was cut down. Black Angus had been a rival of Brutus's father and seemed to relish any opportunity to chastise Brutus, which only made the young warrior more rebellious.

One fateful evening, during the annual attack on the human settlement of Boon's Dock, Brutus was forced to make a choice that would decide, once and for all, whether he would live a life of submission or fully embrace his insubordination.

"Spoiler alert. I'm totally gonna kick that other cow's ass."

"Please tell me Sir Larpsalot and Elvish Presley are staying at an inn in Boon's Dock," Lorenzo said.

Asher shook his head. "No, our heroes' stories do not intersect this auspicious night."

"Seriously?" Lorenzo whined.

Steer Clear's battle trumpets rent the otherwise silent night. It wasn't long before Brutus was performing a deadly dance among the village's woefully weak defenders. Lost in a symphony of carnage, Brutus hardly noticed when one victim fell and another terrified human took its place. All of their faces looked the same.

Until he glimpsed the visage of a man with a twisted

nose and a scar etched across the length of his neck.

A nose once broken by Brutus's father.

A neck that had bled after getting gored by Beau Vine's horn.

Yes, the grizzled veteran across the battlefield—a middle-aged man clad in dented full plate and wielding a serrated sword—was none other than the warrior who had slain the clan chieftain so many years ago.

Asher paused for dramatic effect.

"OK," Mak said, "how do I kill the bastard?"

Bellowing an anguish-filled battle cry, Brutus the Bullheaded thundered across a village green painted red with blood. He barely felt the sting of a guardsman's dagger as it grazed his shoulder, hardly noted the reflexive jab of his battle axe as the spiked tip pierced the insignificant man's face.

"Plan A."

"What?" Asher asked Mak.

"The name of my axe is Plan A," she explained. "Isn't that what you said back at your house?"

Brutus raised the blood-slicked axe above his head. Plan A had seen him through a hundred battles. With his father's weapon in hand, Brutus never needed a Plan B.

Yet the scarred man was no novice himself. He spied Brutus's charge out of the corner of his eye, spun to face his roaring adversary, and easily sidestepped the overhead chop of Plan A.

"Oh, it's on!" Mak declared.

Asher scooped up the broomstick handle Lorenzo had requisitioned for Sir Larpsalot's sword a few sessions back and glowered fiercely at Mak.

"You'll not find me so easy prey, you bestial abomination," spoke the man who had butchered Brutus's father. "Prepare to die!"

Asher swung the broomstick at Mak, not in slow motion but not too fast either, giving her plenty of time to dodge or parry. At first, he thought she was just going to block the attack—as Elvish Presley and Sir Larpsalot would do during their sparring matches—but Mak swung with her full might.

Hockey stick struck broom handle with an echoing thwack, sending the mock sword clattering over the side of the cliff.

Lorenzo groaned. "Now what am I gonna use for a weapon? If I ever get to play again, that is…"

Ignoring Lorenzo, Mak said to Asher, "Now I chop off his head."

The sheer power behind the young minotaur's attack had caught Nikolai the Gnarled off guard.

"His name is Nikolai?" Mak asked incredulously.

"What's wrong with Nikolai the Gnarled?" Asher asked.

"It sounds too cool, and that's better than he deserves," she replied. "How about Norbert?"

The sheer power behind the young minotaur's attack had caught Norbert off guard.

Norbert hadn't survived this long by lingering on an unfavorable battlefield. He knew when he was outmatched. Rather than reach for the dagger at his belt, he turned his back on the people of Boon's Dock and fled into the night.

"I chase after him!" Mak shouted, running toward Asher, her hockey stick once again raised over her head.

Asher took a big step back.

With the taste of vengeance on his tongue, Brutus broke ranks, confident his longer, more muscular legs would easily outpace the armor-laden human. However, before he made it five steps, Black Angus barred his passage.

Asher looked to Lorenzo expectantly.

"So I get to play after all?" he said with a sigh. "But it's a character I know nothing about?"

Asher whispered some key information in Lorenzo's ear while Mak eyed them suspiciously.

"We must take our spoils and go," Black Angus told Brutus. "The townsfolk have hired a company of mercenaries. We have lost five of our herd—"

"Clan," Asher corrected Lorenzo.

"—five of our clan already."

"Brutus says..." Mak started to say, but then she started talking in a lower, guff tone.

Brutus said, "I have finally found the man responsible for my father's death. I *will* have my revenge!"

Black Angus grabbed Brutus by the arm, earning him a baleful look from the younger minotaur. "I am the clan chieftain. You will obey my command!"

"Eat manure," Brutus the Bullheaded growled. He shoved past Black Angus and sprinted after Norbert.

Mak gave Lorenzo a shove, and before either boy could stop her, she disappeared over the edge of the quarry.

Asher ran up to the ledge, fully expecting to find the girl lying like a lifeless ragdoll at the bottom of the pit.

Ten feet below him, Mak looked up from a rocky shelf. She held up the broom handle. "I'm going after Norbert. Is the dude unarmed, or did he grab another sword when he ran off like a little bitch?"

Exhaling a sigh of relief, Asher called down, "He's got a dagger. That's it."

Mak laughed triumphantly and skidded farther down

the steep wall of the quarry, sending a spray of stones skittering down into the massive hole.

"We can't go down there," Lorenzo said softly to Asher. "Just tell her she caught up to Norbert and killed him or whatever."

Asher could have done that—arguably *should* have done that—but noticing a flat, almost stage-like outcropping farther down, he had a sudden idea for this larping session's finale.

"She seems to be doing OK," Asher said, watching Mak navigate the rocky terrain deeper into the quarry.

"It's dangerous," Lorenzo argued.

Still watching Mezzo-Earth's newest adventurer chase her invisible prey, Asher smiled. "Yeah, but danger always makes a story more interesting."

Brutus reached the hidden camp of Steer Clear Clan just before sunrise. His rich brown fur matted with blood, the minotaur acknowledged the sentries, Jersey and Holstein, with a tired grunt.

He was eager for rest, but when a shadow fell over him from behind, he knew he would not avoid a final confrontation before reaching his tent.

"Brutus!" Black Angus cried. "You broke the rules, and by defying my orders, you put the clan in danger."

Without turning to face the chieftain, Brutus said, "I did what I had to do…for my father."

Black Angus snorted. "Your father is at peace. He died a warrior's death many seasons past. Your behavior today dishonored his memory and your entire bloodline."

"Oh no you didn't," Mak mumbled to Lorenzo.

Brutus's eyes narrowed dangerously. "What do you know of honor, Black Angus? What glory have you brought our clan since stepping into my father's shoes?"

Mak paused. "Do minotaurs wear shoes?"

Asher shook his head. "They have hooves."

"What glory have you brought our clan since stepping into my father's hooves?"

"So much worse," Lorenzo whispered.

Black Angus squared his shoulders, then crossed his arms. "You leave me no choice. Because of your insubordination, I hereby banish you from the clan."

"That's bullshit!" Brutus sneered.

All three teens laughed at that one.

"If we see you in our territory again, we will kill you." With that, Black Angus turned his back on the outcast. The sentries followed suit.

"Who put this asshole in charge anyway?" Mak asked Asher.

"He was the strongest warrior in the clan when Beau Vine died. No one challenged him for the title of chieftain."

"I challenge you," Brutus said in a low voice.

Black Angus lurched as though struck from behind. He spun around to cast a withering look at Brutus. "You cannot be serious."

"Deadly serious."

Black Angus laughed. "Trials by combat are fought to the death, Brutus. Are you ready to feed your body to the land and water the grass with your blood?"

"The real question," Brutus replied, "is whether you're ready to be put out to pasture."

"Nice one," Asher said.

"Thanks," Mak replied.

Despite his fatigue from last night's battle and the chase that followed, Brutus felt a sudden surge of conviction. Black Angus was confident, *too* confident. The chieftain was bigger, but Brutus was faster, especially when the older minotaur swung The Prod, his enormous battle hammer.

Plan A had never failed Brutus before. He knew it would not today.

Asher smiled slyly.

Except a minotaur duel would demand a more intimate means of violence—the transparent glass-bladed daggers of Steer Clear Clan's most ancient ceremonies.

Mak looked down at what Asher had just handed to her and Lorenzo. "Why are you giving us granola bars."

"Best I could come up with for daggers."

The battle that followed was the most brutal the clan had seen in generations.

Atop the flat-topped ledge, Mak took a swipe at Lorenzo, who caught her wrist and countered with a jab to her midsection. Mak twisted to avoid the granola bar. The edge of the wrapper grazed her T-shirt.

Although Brutus managed to dodge Black Angus's hungry blade time and time again, the chieftain supplemented each swing with a fist or a foot. Every collision added another bruise to Brutus's poor, punished body.

Lorenzo pantomimed a punch to Mak's cheek, then another to her ribs.

His strength sapped, Brutus could only fend off the deadliest of the assaults and had little offense of his own.

Mak lashed out with her granola bar, which went far wide of Lorenzo's chest. Lorenzo followed up with a stiff-arm that sent the girl backpedaling.

All seemed lost for young Brutus the Bullheaded.

Mak's heel came down past the edge of the stone platform. Her arms pinwheeled as she tried to catch her balance. Mak fell five feet, crumpling at the base of the battle stage.

*　　　*　　　*

"Mak!"

Asher shared a panicked look with Lorenzo before scrambling over to their unmoving friend. Kneeling beside her, he gently rolled Mak onto her back. An angry red gash above her eyebrow dripped blood down the side of her face.

"Is she OK?" Lorenzo asked, still perched atop the stone shelf.

"I…I don't know…she's breathing…"

"Is that *blood*?" Before Asher could answer, Lorenzo added, "I *told* you this was a bad idea."

Asher brushed some of the quarry dust from Mak's arm, but her skin remained white from the fresh scrape— white flecked with red. The girl didn't flinch.

He looked up at Lorenzo. "We need to get help."

"No," someone whispered.

Asher gasped and turned back to Mak. Had she spoken, or was his mind playing tricks on him? Eyes closed, Mak still appeared to be knocked out cold.

"She could have a concussion or something," Asher told Lorenzo. "I'll stay with her. You climb out and bike to the nearest house."

"No," the whisper returned, "get him to come down here."

This time, Asher was quick enough to see Mak's lips move as she breathed the words "down here."

"What?" he asked.

Mak sighed, opening one eye. "Haven't you ever heard of playing possum?"

"Is she awake?" Lorenzo called down.

Mak's mouth curled into a half smile. Quietly, she said, "Black Angus is a lot stronger than Brutus, right?"

Relief and confusion scrambling his thoughts, Asher found himself answering automatically. "He's on a much higher level, and he had a short rest while you were battling Norbert."

"Right," Mak whispered. "Which is why I gotta trick him."

By this point, Lorenzo had reached the bottom of the quarry. "Mak, are you…"

Mak sprang forward, knocking Lorenzo onto his back. Straddling his chest, she pressed the edge of her granola bar under the boy's chin and slowly drew the jagged wrapper across his neck.

After a moment of stunned silence, Lorenzo said, "Wow."

Wiping blood from the side of her face, Mak said, "Even with one eye, Brutus is a beast!"

Holstein, Jersey, and the rest of the gathered minotaurs gazed in reverent silence as Brutus the Bullheaded slit Black Angus's throat.

Then the warriors erupted in shouts of celebration, hailing Brutus the victor and new leader of the Steer Clear Clan.

"You should loot the body," Lorenzo told Mak.

"What do you mean?"

"Sometimes enemies have valuable gear on them," Lorenzo explained. "And Asher likes giving bosses the good stuff."

Mak looked at Asher. "I want to do the looting thing."

Despite the deafening cries around him, Brutus heard a low, rumbling voice inside his head. At first, he feared Black Angus had somehow survived the finishing blow. But when he looked down at his fallen enemy, the only sign of life he saw was the strange pulsing of the copper bracelet wrapped around Black Angus's bicep.

The voice seemed to come from the curled piece of metal.

"Brutus," the Tuff Cuff called. "I have been worn by every chieftain of this clan, and now, by right, I am yours."

Brutus bent down and pulled the copper bangle off the dead minotaur's arm. He never heard the talisman talk again, but he would always remember how the Tuff Cuff seemed to speak with the voice of his father.

"Three cheers for the new chieftain!" Holstein shouted.

The warriors of Steer Clear Clan raised tankards and wineskins in toast to their new leader.

"So I'm the boss now?" Mak asked.

"If that's what you want," Asher said. *"I didn't think you'd actually win."*

"Wait...I was supposed to die?"

Asher smiled. "No. The Goddess of the Stampede would have shielded you from the killing blow. Or maybe Black Angus would have let you live, broken and disgraced."

"But if Brutus stays with the clan, he'll never meet Sir Larpsalot and Elvish Presley," Lorenzo protested. *"I mean, we could definitely use some extra muscle in the party."*

Asher hid a smile and shrugged. "It's up to Mak. If she wants to keep playing, we'll find a way. But if she doesn't, this is a fine ending for Brutus the Bullheaded."

He risked a glance at Mak, who took a big bite out of her granola bar.

*   *   *

The ride back to Asher's house took longer than the trek to the quarry had. Climbing up the steep sides of the gorge had been more work than any of them anticipated. Now Asher's legs ached as he pedaled along the highway. Countless scratches adorned his arms and knees.

But he didn't care. He couldn't remember ever having so much fun larping.

Even Lorenzo wore a grin as they coasted down the driveway and up to the old farmhouse. Jabber greeted them with excited barks, tugging against his lead. Mak eased her bike over to the dog, who lifted his head for some much-needed chin scratches.

"Do you want to come in and clean up?" Asher asked her. "We have some bandages…"

Mak shot him a smirk. "Nah. I'm good."

"What are you gonna to tell your parents…about what happened?" Lorenzo asked.

Mak wheeled over to them. "That some mean boy pushed me off a cliff."

"What?" Lorenzo exclaimed. "It was an accident, and I already said I'm—"

She cut him off with a laugh. "Relax, Lopez. I get more roughed up on the ice. No one will probably even notice one more scar. See you guys next time."

"Next time"—the words filled Asher with so much excitement he feared his chest might explode.

Hockey stick in one hand, her other on the handlebars, Mak rode away. Over her shoulder, she said, "And Asher?"

"Yeah?"

"Thanks for inviting me."

Beside him, Lorenzo leaned his bike against the house and said, "I'm going to try to get some of this dust off of me. If I'm lucky, my parents won't ever figure out we went into the quarry."

Asher let him go. His mind was already weaving a bizarre set of circumstances that would place Brutus—self-exiled and eager for new challenges—in the path of a certain human paragon and elvish minstrel.

Watching Mak vanish around the bend, Asher knew the encounter would change the lives of all three of them forever.

Flesh & Blood

Snow lunged for cover an instant before he consciously recognized the gunfire for what it was. Following a haphazard somersault, he slammed his back up against a narrow filing cabinet, just in time to hear another shot. Small craters in the opposite wall peppered him with plaster.

It wasn't the first time his reflexes—honed to a practically superhuman level—had saved his life.

But judging from the deep chuckle across the room, it could damn well be the last. He knew that laugh. Shit.

"Returning to the crime scene?" the other man taunted. "That's just sloppy, Snow."

His body on autopilot, Snow fired two rounds at the direction of the voice. The abbreviated hiss of the silencer centered his thoughts, bought him a couple seconds to come up with a plan.

"It's not what you think, Turk," he called over his shoulder, his even tone echoing off the empty walls of the small office.

The other man chuckled again but not loud enough to mask the sound of a shotgun getting reloaded.

"Right. And killing you won't bring Osprey and the others back," Turk said. "But it'll make me feel *so* much better."

The third blast from the shotgun hit the filing cabinet. A thin sheet of metal and whatever was inside the thing saved him from a spine full of lead. Depending on how many shells Turk had on him, Snow knew his flimsy cover couldn't protect him much longer.

"Think about it," he yelled. "What do I have to gain from offing the Flock…from offing *Oz*?"

"Dunno. Lovers' quarrel, maybe?" Turk punctuated the question with another boom from the shotgun.

Snow was already moving, though, as the filing cabinet slammed into the wall behind him. Rolling on his stomach, he fired at Turk—or where he assumed the other assassin stood—but Turk had already ducked down behind an overturned table.

From his new position behind a sturdy desk, Snow said, "I know *I'm* not the traitor, and I'm pretty sure it's not you either."

"No?"

"No," Snow replied. "Mostly 'cause you're not smart enough to pull this off. Which means we've been set up by an outsider."

"Impossible," Turk argued, his low voice rumbling.

Snow held the barrel of his pistol parallel against his chest. "It's the only explanation."

"Unless *you're* the traitor."

Snow rolled his eyes. He knew from the first gunshot his chances of talking his way out of this were skeleton-slim. After he identified his attacker, negotiation seemed even less likely. The guy called himself Turkey Vulture for Christ's sake, and he wasn't known for his reasoning skills.

Death was the only way this encounter could end.

"I suppose swearing on a stack of Bibles won't change your mind?" Snow asked.

Turk's bear-growl laugh was answer enough.

So be it, Snow thought.

He popped up as if he was going to shoot but crouched back down just as quickly. The shotgun fired. Snow sprang over the desk, yelling as he fired in quick succession at Turk, who dropped behind the overturned table. Snow had hoped the big man would've fired his second shot, maybe winging him at worst. No such luck. Now he was at close range with one shot left in his pistol.

And the single shell in Turk's shotgun gave the other assassin the advantage at such close range.

Guess I'll be seeing you in Hell, Oz.

The teeth-jarring collision of his shoulder against the table rattled all other thoughts from his skull. His momentum was enough to pin Turk between the wooden tabletop and the wall, but the metal legs, combined with his opponent's considerable bulk, prevented him from scoring any serious damage.

Still, the maneuver accomplished what Snow intended. His arms down at his sides, instinctively pushing against the improvised trap, Turk couldn't raise his shotgun. But neither could Snow stop pushing long enough to aim his own weapon.

It might've been a stalemate, except for the fact that Turk had fifty pounds of muscle on him.

"Stupid move, Snow." The table between them edged closer to him, scraping loudly against the floor and pushing Snow back a couple of inches. "Time to kiss your white ass goodbye."

Here goes nothing.

Snow shifted his weight suddenly, pulling back from the table. The full brunt of Turk's shove launched the table into him. He used his left arm to deflect as much of the force as he could while raising his gun at Turk.

However, he couldn't maintain his balance.

He was falling, and the second he hit the ground, Turk would discharge his last round into his chest.

Snow squeezed his trigger.

The shotgun answered.

Snow's head struck the floor with a thud, which didn't help the ringing in his ears whatsoever. He waited for the adrenaline or shock or whatever to subside, braced for the agony of his fatal wound to seep in.

When the pain didn't come, he rolled onto his side, reloaded by reflex, and pointed the tip of his silencer at the table. Turk's rushed shot had missed him somehow, but the other hitman could be readying to fire again from cover.

Whereas Snow was screwed, lying out in the open.

"It doesn't have to go down like this," Snow said, watching for any sign of movement behind the table, any excuse to fire.

No reply.

Slowly, his aim never faltering, Snow rose to his feet. "Turk?"

Silence.

Carefully stepping forward, he stopped just shy of the table. Then with a burst of speed, he craned his arm over the edge and fired two shots. When Turk failed to cry out or pop up like some murderous jack-in-the-box, Snow shoved the table aside.

His most recent shots had missed any vital areas, but not the desperate one he had fired while falling, which had just missed Turk's left eye, punching through his temple and into his brain.

"God damn you for making me do that," he muttered.

Snow took a few steps back and leaned against the disheveled desk until his pulse slowed to a less painful pace. Although he would live to kill another day, Snow felt anything but lucky. The torn-up office around him was a perfect metaphor for the Flock's fate. Whoever had systematically murdered his brothers in arms—and inadvertently instigated the pointless showdown between him and Turk—was still out there somewhere.

Turning his attention to the overturned filing cabinet, Snow vowed to discover the Flock's hidden enemy and avenge his dear Oz.

Osprey steps into the church, glances at the golden cruci-fix beyond the rows of pews, and frowns.

He's never had much use for churches—not before his father walked into one, never to be seen again, and certainly not after. He reflects how everything from the fool's-gold filigree coating the architecture to the omni-present whiff of incense in the air reeks of inauthenticity. Counterfeit comfort. A promise destined to be broken.

But a job's a job, and the Flock can't afford to look weak. Reputation is as much a currency as the digits in a bank account—maybe even more so because Osprey can't improve the latter without repairing the former.

Things went from bad to worse after Kingfisher's disappearance. If he doesn't turn things around, his legacy will be one stained with failure, and the organization his father worked so hard to build will crumble as a result of his mysterious death.

The first of many mysterious deaths.

Step one is staying alive long enough to finish the mission, collect his pay, and hope his contractor spreads the word about the Flock's renewed respect. It's Osprey's only play.

He scans the sanctuary, looking for any signs of life.

"Over here, my son."

His hand flies to the holster at his hip, but he doesn't draw. The voice came from a nearby confessional. While Osprey doesn't relish the idea of confining himself in the tomb-for-two, he straightens his suit coat—his "*Pulp Fiction* bullshit," as Snow calls it—and walks over to the polished wooden structure. He's tempted to kick open the door, drag his employer out by his silly white collar, and put an end to the cloak-and-dagger routine.

Then again, he thinks, the priest probably associates the confessional with sin, so why not place an order for murder from inside the secretive space?

One hand lingering near his hip, Osprey opens the creaky door. Stifling a sigh, he sits down and closes it behind him, ushering in a heavy darkness.

"Is this the part where I say, 'Bless me, Father, for I am about to sin?' Or are you looking for a little role reversal?"

Every nerve in Osprey's body protests when the small window slides open, revealing the silhouette of his latest employer behind the shadowy screen.

"Are you always so sarcastic with your clients?" the priest asks.

By his voice alone, Osprey identifies the man as landing somewhere between middle-aged and elderly. He's black—not that Osprey cares. Money is green no matter whose hand holds it, though he has to admit he'd rather kill white folks than his own kind. As for who's paying him, who cares?

"Sorry, Father," Osprey says, reminding himself that every gig helps rebuild the Flock's rep and that pissing off a priest is, at best, counterproductive. "I'm all ears. Just tell me who needs to die."

The sigh on the other side of the wooden wall is

steeped in emotion. Regret? No, resignation. The priest isn't going to change his mind. He's just sad that it has come to this. Osprey shrugs inwardly. Level-headed clients are always easier to work with. Less worry about a braggart blabbing what his dirty dollars bought or succumbing to a tardy conscience.

"My son," the priest says, nearly whispering.

Osprey almost prompts him to continue, mistaking the words for an impersonal address. But no, he realizes suddenly, the priest is asking him to kill his own flesh-and-blood—and likely illegitimate—son.

"Do you want to know why?" the priest asks.

Osprey shakes his head, remembers the other man can't see him, and says, "Doesn't matter."

"Ah, but it matters to me."

Very well, Osprey thinks. Spill your guts, old man.

"I have made many mistakes in my life," the priest says. "We're all sinful creatures, of course, and when I think of the things I've done...but my greatest regret is how bad I failed my son. Because of who I was...and what I wanted to become...I couldn't be the father he deserved. As a result, he grew up to be a terrible person."

Osprey nods to himself, eager to get to the important stuff. "How do you want it done?"

A wry chuckle wafts through the window between them. "Quickly. Painlessly. But I know that isn't possible."

"You'd be surprised," Osprey says, trying to be helpful.

"Maybe. But I doubt he'll go down without a fight."

Osprey frowns. "Why, does he know I'm coming?"

"No, but he should," the priest replies. "I've been offing his friends for months now."

*   *   *

Snow slammed the sheet of paper down onto the desk. The sound ricocheted off the empty white walls.

He'd just found a clue. He was as certain of that as he had been certain of his movements during Turk's ambush.

But what did it mean?

Three hours spent in the Flock's hidden headquarters —disguised as the dreary habitat of a common pencil-pusher—had taken him through reams of paper meant for the eyes of one man only. Kingfisher had kept careful records, and when Osprey inherited the right to rule the roost from his father, he had tried to do the same.

Unfortunately, neither Snow nor, apparently, Osprey had been able to make sense of Kingfisher's cypher.

"The old man was paranoid…and too damn smart for his own good," Snow told Turk.

The corpse of his colleague deigned not to reply.

"Oz, on the other hand," Snow continued, "he's no dummy, but I was able to crack his code in ten minutes flat. Which means I've been able to learn a few things, including the fact that no one has retired from the Flock since Kingfisher's disappearance. No, they were all killed. Oz did a damn fine job of covering that up. Probably didn't want to scare us, eh?"

Turk continued to keep his opinions to himself.

"But this…" Snow picked up the page again. "This is Oz's last mission. A church in Trenton. I have no proof, but I'd bet ten large it's the same one Kingfisher walked into the day he vanished."

He could almost hear Turk's reply: "But what's so special about some church in New Jersey?"

"I don't know…yet." Snow stood, stretched, and scratched an itch that mirrored the one in his mind. "I'm sure you won't mind if I take my leave and do a little investigating."

Deciding against taking Turk's double-barreled shotgun—Snow preferred a subtler style—he spent the next few minutes pouring gasoline over the Flock's records. He supposed the jerrycan had been stashed in the corner of the room for that very purpose. Why bother with digital files and firewalls when you can destroy your secrets with actual fire?

With one final glance back at the remnants of Kingfisher's empire and Osprey's birthright, Snow dropped the match. A whoosh of heat hit his back as he walked away.

"Enjoy your funeral pyre, Turk. It's time I went to church."

Eyes wide, muscles clenched, Osprey waits for the priest to explain himself. Waits for the old man's words to make some kind of sense. Or, at least, to form a meaning beyond what he thinks he already understands.

"I've missed you so much, Oz."

As soon as the last word leaves the priest's mouth, Osprey dives forward. He crashes through the flimsy wooden door, rolls to his feet, and aims his gun at the other side of the confessional.

Common sense demands for him to fire until his clip is empty, filling the glorified closet with holes at varying elevations. Killing his father before the infamous Kingfisher, self-professed slayer of assassins, kills him.

Two things stop him from shooting. One, his father could've killed him the second he sat down in the fresh-polished deathtrap. And two, Osprey has to know why Kingfisher did what he did.

"Come on out...*slowly*," he demands.

He might have been worried about someone else responding to the ruckus—another clergyman or some church lady squandering her Saturday there—but he knows Kingfisher is too careful to allow for any witnesses. Osprey would've bet Snow's dog tags, a recent gift and his most prized possession, that his father rigged the front door to lock behind him.

It's just us, he thinks sourly. Father, son, and holy hell.

Osprey is about to repeat his command when the other door of the confessional swings open. A man who looks like his father but also a complete stranger steps out. Osprey can almost convince himself the guy is a long-lost uncle and that his father's twin chose the cloth over the clip.

But no. This is Kingfisher. Older and, if his earlier declaration is to be believed, even deadlier than before.

"*Why?*" It's the only word he can pry from his own lips.

Kingfisher breathes another sigh and, apparently unperturbed by Osprey's gun, wanders over to the nearest pew to sit down. "It's a long story, Oz."

A rush of heat washes over Osprey's face. He wishes he could be as cool and collected as Snow always seems to be. Doing his best to ignore the thundering in his chest, Osprey marches over to the pew.

Gun pointed at his father's head, he says, "Give me the abridged edition."

Kingfisher smiles that unique smile of his—not so much a curving upward of the lips as a horizontal stretch, a *widening* of the mouth. "Ten years ago, I was hired to kill a priest. It was a job, just like any other. Or so I thought. I'd killed so many people, seen that look of terror in their eyes when they realize their time has come.

"But this mark…this *priest*…was different."

Even though his arm is starting to stiffen, Osprey keeps the barrel pointed at his father's face.

"No fear," Kingfisher continues. "None whatsoever. It's so strange, so *unnerving*, that I hesitated, giving him time to speak his final words…'I forgive you.'"

The old man's voice cracks. He looks down at his hands.

"So, what then?" Osprey asks. "You chicken out and swear you'll never kill an innocent man again?"

"No." His father looks up. "No, I shot him between the eyes. He died instantly. I killed the customer too. If you'd have asked me then why I did it, I wouldn't have been able to tell you. It took a while, months, before I could accept the truth."

"Which is?"

Kingfisher shrugs. "That I'm damned."

Osprey throws his hands up and scoffs. "You've lost your goddamned mind."

"No, it's my *soul* that's lost," Kingfisher argues. "My mind has never been clearer."

Osprey lowers his gun to his side but doesn't holster it. "So you saw the light? Time to wash your hands of professional murder and make nice with God, is that it?"

"Yes, I asked Him for forgiveness, but as time went on, I realized that if I were to truly atone for my actions, I'd have to rid the world of the evil I created. My wickedness was nurtured by blood. So, then, my redemption should be borne of it."

"No," Osprey says, "I was right the first time. You've lost your—"

"No!" Kingfisher is on his feet and in Osprey's face before he can raise his gun. "If you had seen what I saw…if you had *experienced* all I have experienced since joining the church, you'd understand."

Osprey doubts it, but he says nothing. His father is within striking distance, and even though Osprey knows he's stronger than Kingfisher, he knows better than to underestimate the man.

"And you called me here, why?" Osprey asks. "To kill me like you killed the others? To off your own kid and tip the divine scales further in your favor?"

The intensity in his father's eyes is almost enough to make him drop his gun in surprise.

"I'm sorry, son. If the Flock is to die, then Osprey must die too."

Snow lingered in the back of the sanctuary long after the last of the congregation left the church.

It took him more than half of the homily to convince himself he wasn't hallucinating. Now, watching the priest say goodbye to his fellow clergymen, he couldn't deny the identity of the preacher—the familiar gestures, the bright smile few people ever used to see.

He willed his pulse to slow once more. His old drill sergeant had called what he did "biofeedback," but for Snow it was always just focusing his thoughts, *commanding* his body to obey his will. He often used the technique for dulling pain.

Physical pain anyway.

At the front of the church, the priest removed his white robe, folded it, and set it on the altar. "You can come out now if you like. We're alone."

Snow didn't bother to retreat further into the shadows. The man was a professional. He had likely spotted Snow soon after he joined the flow of people into the church. There was nothing left to do now but follow the strip of carpet to the front of the church and confront his not-dead boyfriend.

"Snow," greeted the priest. "I was wondering how long it would take you to find me."

"Oz," Snow replied, not allowing his mouth to smile or frown. "You mind telling me what the hell is going on here?"

"It's kind of a long story."

"Give me the abridged edition."

The man formerly known as Osprey and currently called Father Byrd laughed softly. "Yeah, that's what I said."

Oz the Priest didn't move from his place behind the altar as he spoke, and not once during his ex's speech did Snow consider taking his hand off the handle of his pistol. In fact, he wished he had brought Turk's shotgun along for reconnaissance, as impractical as that would have been on a busy Sunday morning.

Anyway, he didn't want to kill Oz, not unless he had to. And for a moment—despite the warning buzzing in the back of his mind—he thought it wouldn't come to that, not after hearing how it had been Kingfisher, hiding out here as a priest for nearly a decade, who had clipped the wings of the Flock, one by one.

But his fingertip found its way to the trigger when Oz admitted to picking up where his father left off the past few months.

"So you two are in this together, huh?" Snow asked, unable to steady the trembling in his voice.

"No," Oz said softly. "Not in the way you think any-way. I killed Kingfisher in this very church. Thought I had to. Hell, he *wanted* me to. And in that moment I saw in his eyes what he must have seen in that other priest's eyes…"

"And what's that?"

Oz had the audacity to smile. "Peace."

"I think I get it," Snow said slowly. "Kingfisher's legacy was already in the toilet when you found him here, so you decided to finish what he started? You couldn't *succeed* as the leader of the Flock, so why not tear down the rest of what your daddy built?"

Oz sighed. "Not exactly."

Snow drew his gun but didn't aim yet. "Then why don't you spell it out for me, Oz or Father Byrd or whoever the hell you are these days?"

"Watching my father bleed out, staring down at his peaceful face, I understood what it was he had discovered years ago. Redemption is better than money or notoriety or the rush you get from a kill or—"

"Or *us*?" Snow asked. The last word echoed off the rafters.

Oz closed his eyes. "Yes. I'm sorry...but yes."

"Well, this isn't the first time I've been told I don't deserve happiness."

Oz frowned. "You don't understand—"

"No, I don't!" Snow's voice boomed as he took a step closer to the altar, closer to Oz. "Because you're too smart to believe this crazy crusade makes any kind of sense, and you had to know I would find you, which means you must want to die. Or you plan to finish off the Flock right here and now."

"Turkey Vulture?" Oz asked.

"Idiot tried to kill me. So it's just Osprey and Snowy Owl...two birds of a feather once...and now an endangered species, thanks to you to and your crazy old man."

Oz leaned forward against the altar, one hand clasping the cloth on top and the other hand out down of view.

"I don't want to kill you, Snow."

"A part of me feels the same way," he replied. "But another part me would love nothing more than to watch you die."

That same part imagined the hitman-turned-minister reaching for a piece behind the altar. And it dared him to make a move, *prayed* he would.

Snow stared at his adversary for the longest sixty seconds of his life. Oz stared back.

"Do you ever give your marks the chance to say any last words?" Oz finally asked him.

"Nuh-uh. You?"

"Nope." Oz brought his other hand up from behind the altar. "But just so you know, I forgive—"

Snow fired.

Oz dropped to the floor, an empty candlestick holder rolling from his lifeless hand.

Unparalleled

I was sitting on the toilet when the men with guns barged into my bathroom.

Silver lining: I wasn't dropping a deuce. I always sit down to pee—not because it makes less of a mess than standing or because I have anyone to impress with a spotless commode. Truth is, I'm just lazy. Besides, that minute or two in the bathroom could be spent catching up on social media or doing a level in whatever mobile game I was addicted to at the moment.

Which is all to say that at least a need for TP wasn't vying for my attention when the lead gunman yanked me off my porcelain throne. I might've said, "What?" or "Who?" Whichever question fragment spilled out of my mouth was quickly converted into a cry of alarm and fear. Tripped up by my jeans, I fell forward into the arms of the black-clad soldier. He spun me around roughly, forcing my arms behind me. An echoing click confirmed what I thought I felt. The guy had just cuffed me.

I might've pissed my pants if I hadn't just gone—or if I'd been wearing pants.

Humiliated and horrified, I'm pretty sure I managed to say, "What's going on?" before the gag wrapped around my face, filling my mouth with a synthetic, salty flavor. Despite the toothpaste spatters on the mirror, I got a good look at the small army of bathroom invaders. Their gear—helmets sporting opaque visors and body armor bereft of any insignias—told me jack shit about their identities or intentions. As the first gunman freed me from my bunched-up boxers, jeans, and any hope of dignity, the second guy aimed a black pistol with a dull finish at my nose.

The final infiltrator kept his back to us, pointing the scariest machine gun I've ever seen into the hall toward my living room. As though Horace, the laziest housecat on Earth, was about to come to my rescue.

I struggled. I yelled incoherently into the gag. I winced as the leader's talon-like fingers dug into a pressure point between my neck and shoulder.

Don't get me wrong. I knew I wasn't going to get away. But instinct is a funny thing. I'd heard that in times of distress, there's fight, flight, and maybe even freeze. A new F-word came to me as a sudden dizziness scrambled my thoughts:

Faint.

When I woke, I could almost convince myself the strange scene had been a dream, possibly brought on by one too many chill pills or bad Thai takeout.

No chance of that. This wasn't the comfortable darkness of my bedroom, crooked blinds barely managing to block out the relentless lights of the apartment parking lot. Nope, the suffocating shade was a direct result of something covering my head. Another surge of denial might have been enough to convince me it was just a pillow and that Horace was undoubtedly curled up at the bottom of my bed, except I knew I was sitting upright.

Tied to a stiff-backed chair God-knows-where in the

custody of God-knows-who.

The soggy gag absorbed most of my whimper. While I'd never mistaken myself for a brave man, nothing in the past thirty-four years had prepared me for how powerful a force fear could be. The closest I had ever come to this ice-cold, shivery feeling was back in high school when Aaron Wendell, in all his Slipknot T-shirt glory, had promised to deliver a beating after eighth hour. The anxiety-drenched anticipation had been so much worse than the series of shoves that sent me to the ground and ripped a perfectly good pair of pants.

Recalling my Black Ops assailants, I doubted I'd be so lucky this time around.

The same questions as before swirled in my brain. Who were those soldiers? Why did they kidnap me from my cookie-cutter suburban apartment? What could they possibly want with a nobody like me?

Over the next five to five hundred minutes, I ran through a series of scenarios, each less likely than the one before it:

A crime syndicate specializing in organ harvesting had set their sights on my kidneys.

Someone I knew had made an enemy of the Mafia.

Domestic terrorists wanted to show Middle America it was far from safe, starting with an IT middle manager from Wisconsin.

Shaking my head didn't dislodge the hood. Pulling against whatever secured my wrists to the arms of the chair only caused them to dig deeper into my skin. My tongue hurt from trying to dislodge the gag.

Eventually, fear faded into annoyance, giving way to boredom—and hunger. How long had I been sitting there? Long enough to convince myself that whatever came next couldn't be worse than waiting.

Of course, the instant a sound interrupted the absolute silence around me, I was wishing for the blessed boredom of before. A door had opened. Echoing footsteps grew louder. Multiple pairs of boots striking a concrete floor, or so I assumed. One of the new arrivals said something softly, but I couldn't hope to hear it over the dubstep track thumping in my chest.

Someone tore the thing off my head. I never figured out exactly what it was because my wide-eyed stare was pulled first to a pair of super-sized assault rifles and then the men in black body armor toting them. If these were the same men as from my apartment, they had traded in the third member of the team for a white woman with curly black hair tied up in a style I'd always thought of as "sexy secretary."

But this was no secretary, judging by the holster peeking out from the jacket of her gray power suit. Her no-nonsense expression couldn't compete for my attention against the crimson of her perfectly full lips. The faintest suggestion of cleavage lurked above her silky black shirt.

Beyond all reason, I was turned on, which immediately made me wonder how apparent that would be, given that half of my outfit had been left back in Brookfield.

To my relief, somebody had covered my lower half with a pair of baggy, navy-blue sweatpants, though the flexible material did little to hide my boner.

If my attractive interrogator noticed the physical response to her proximity, she was kind enough not to mention it. She leaned in closer—the view only exacerbating my erection situation—and studied my face. Her gaze landed somewhere north of my brow.

"Shepherd," she whispered. Taking a step back, she looked me in the eye and said, "How did you get that scar?"

It took me a couple of seconds to make sense of what she was saying. The way she'd said "shepherd" made it sound like a swearword. And the question about my scar—an inch-and-a-half beige line against my otherwise brown skin by my hairline—made no sense.

"I fell." I had to clear my throat to recognize my own voice. "When I was twelve or thirteen…wiped out on my bike."

"Incredible." She brought a finger up to an earpiece I noticed for the first time. "Yes, I noticed that too. Appropriate…and perhaps poetic."

Strapped to a chair in a big garage that was empty except for an SUV speckled with some kind of urban-gray camouflage—*not* an abandoned Mafia warehouse or a command-center basement of a democracy-hating terrorist cell—I couldn't find anything at all poetic about my situation.

"What do you want from me?" I asked, sounding weak and pathetic even to myself.

Rather than answer me, she turned to Shadow Soldier 1 and said, "Remove his restraints."

"Ma'am?" The question came from Shadow Soldier 2, though the unenthusiastic pace of his partner echoed his uncertainty.

"You have your orders," the woman told them. With her finger on the earpiece, she added, "This is *my* operation, Jackson. You observe at my invitation only. Don't make me regret the kindness."

I watched the severed plastic straps fall to the ground and rubbed my wrists. "Thank you."

It was directed at my beautiful liberator, not Shadow Soldier 1, but she had already turned her back to me. "Please follow me."

I obeyed. What choice did I have? Keeping a hand on

the waistband of the one-size-too-large sweatpants, I tried to make sense of my surroundings. The sterile yet scuffed-up corridor, complete with cameras at every corner, screamed military building. Or was "complex" a better term? I couldn't hope to remember the winding path we took from the garage, through three reinforced doors, each with a scanner that read the woman's upraised palm, to a small room that could just as easily serve as a benign meeting space as an impromptu interrogation room.

Never did I forget the shadow soldiers with the next-gen guns keeping pace a few feet behind me.

"Wait out here," she told the gunmen.

"Ma'—?" Shadow Soldier 2 cut himself off. The glare she had sent his way looked deadlier than the weapon he cradled.

She closed the door behind us, gestured toward the high-backed leather chairs, and said, "Please have a seat, Mr. Horn."

Again, I did as I was told. No delusions here. I had no power. She was in charge. She was also my best hope for getting back to my boring life in the burbs—because by my best guess I'd been brought to some secret FBI or CIA facility in Milwaukee.

"Can I get you something to drink?" she asked. "The coffee is dire, but we have Mox."

I'd never heard of Mox. It didn't sound appetizing in the least. "I'm more interested in answers."

Her smile didn't soften her all-business demeanor in the slightest. "I will tell you what I can, Mr. Horn, but we are dealing with a matter of global security. Many of the details are classified."

"Alex," I said, stopping just shy of adding, "Mr. Horn is my father's name."

She chuckled, and I thought I detected some genuine

humor there. "All right, Alex. My name is Domain Sub-marshal Lucier."

She paused, as though waiting for me to say something.

"That's a mouthful" was all I managed.

Her smile twitched. "You can call me Colette."

Beautiful name for a beautiful woman, I thought. Which was stupid. Given the terrifying circumstances, hooking up with a domain submarshal—whatever *that* was—should've been the last thing on my mind. What was it about this lady that had me so distracted?

Fortunately, I wasn't crazy enough to voice anything close to flirty.

"Nice to meet you…I mean, yeah…unless you need me to troubleshoot your iPad, I don't see how I can be of any help to…whatever this is."

She removed her glasses, folded them, and put them in her breast pocket. For the first time I noticed a badge-like pin on her lapel. The colors were patriotic enough, but something about the proportions seemed strange. Or maybe it was the four-pointed star that was throwing me.

Colette seemed to be collecting her thoughts as she stared into my soul. "What I need you to do, Alex, is accompany me to the grid-forsaken compound of the world's most dangerous man and help me infiltrate the most technologically advanced lock I've ever encountered before any foreign power or rival criminal enterprises learn of its location."

I waited for the punchline and was left disappointed.

"Say what?"

"It shouldn't be difficult."

Will it be dangerous? I wondered, but I kept my mouth shut. Sure, I was a coward, but she didn't need to know that.

Instead, I said, "That sounds more difficult than a frozen iPad."

Ignoring me, she replied, "If all goes according to plan, we will return you to your home in less than 24 hours."

And if it *doesn't* go according to plan?

I cleared my throat again, wishing I'd taken her up on her offer for some Mox, and asked, "Sure, I'll help you, but, seriously, *why me*?"

Colette looked down at her hands and, not meeting my eyes, said, "I can't tell you everything. Shep, I can't tell you much of *anything*. Suffice it to say, we need your DNA."

I pulled out an eyelash. "Here ya go."

The smile she gave me was the same kind teachers used to give poor, dumb Aaron Wendell. "As I said before, the security system is incredibly evolved. The lock requires DNA derived from blood…*fresh* blood."

"Who is this guy, Dracula?" I joked.

She didn't laugh.

"You don't need to concern yourself with his identity. In fact, it may give you some comfort to know that he is deceased. We will do our best to shield you from any latent…well…traps. All you need to do is come along for the ride and donate a bit of blood."

"And I'll return home a hero," I said, not bothering to hide my skepticism.

"More or less."

If the devil liked to hide in the details, I envisioned the legions of Hell lurking in the periphery of what could very well end up being Operation Human Sacrifice. I wanted to know what would happen if I refused.

No, actually I didn't. If this covert agency had no compunction against pulling Johnny Q. Public from his bathroom against his will in broad daylight, I'd be going to this supervillain's secret lair whether I liked it or not.

Recalling the salty, chemical taste of the gag, I decided I'd rather participate willingly.

"OK, I'll do it on one condition."

Her arched eyebrows told me she didn't buy my bluff. Regardless, she waved a hand as if to say, "Out with it."

"I need to know why my DNA is the key to this blood lock."

As her stare bore into me again, I wanted to confess my every sin to her—from the lie of omission that veiled the fact that my bike accident was because I stupidly put my feet in the front spokes while riding, to the lusty thoughts I'd been entertaining about her for the past fifteen minutes.

Finally, she opened her mouth, but she didn't get any farther than the word "because" before she pulled the earpiece out and threw it across the room. "Flux you, Jackson. I said I've *got* this!"

After a steadying breath—during which I held mine—she finished: "Because you have the exact same DNA as *our* Alexander Horn."

An hour after leaving Chicago from an airport inexplicably named McCampbell International Airport, I found myself pondering how it was possible I possessed not only the same name, but also the same genetic material as the world's greatest criminal no one ever heard of.

I'd already dismissed the idea of a long-lost twin. Even if identical brothers shared DNA—and I didn't know if that was even true—my parents wouldn't have had any reason to hide a sibling from me.

I took a sip of Mox. The crackly liquid inside the burnt-orange can was a bitterer cola than what I was used to. If

I wasn't struggling with bigger questions, I might have wondered where the U.S. government was getting their off-brand beverages.

Colette sat across a small table from me, reclined nonchalantly in her soft-leather seat. I nearly interrupted her report-reading time to inquire about clones. But why bother? I had pressed her for more information back at her base and during takeoff. All I had gotten in response was an expressionless shake of her head.

He had to be a clone, though. Or *I* was. What other explanation was there?

Conspiracy theories thrashed around my head like piranhas in a goldfish bowl. I glanced across the small jet's only aisle but knew better than to ask Shadow Soldier 1 or 2 for their opinions. The pair remained hidden behind their solid black helmets. For all I knew they were robots. It made as much sense as anything today.

A few minutes later, Colette dropped the manilla folder onto the table, removed her glasses, and took a drink from a glass containing Mox mixed with something stronger. It smelled like whiskey.

"Maker's and Mox," she said, as though reading my mind. "I'd offer you a cocktail, but alcohol could compromise Horn's security system."

Hearing her refer to the *other* Alexander Horn made my skin crawl. Still, I craved more info about my evil twin. "So…how did he die?"

She hesitated but eventually said, "A raid gone wrong. We…well…kind of blew him up."

My soda went down the wrong pipe, sending me into a coughing fit.

Colette smirked. "More accurately, we forced his hand, and he apparently blew *himself* up. We were able to obtain his DNA from the scene but no viable blood…not that we could have transported it to his primary base of operations in time to fool the system."

"What kind of guy was he? I mean, what did he do to make the Earth's Most Wanted list?"

"What *didn't* he do?" she muttered before polishing off her drink.

Pressing my luck, I asked, "Why have I never heard of a mega-terrorist with the same name as me?"

She leaned forward as though about to tell me a secret. I mimicked the move. Her words tickled my ears: "I guess you just need to get out more."

I sniffed. "Yeah, when this is all over, we'll hit a bar at the McCampbell airport, and the Maker's and Moxes are on me."

"M&Ms," she said.

"Like the candy?" I asked.

"What candy?"

I turned away from her. "You like messing with me, huh?"

Her deep, throaty laugh surprised me only slightly less than my unexpected company in the bathroom that morning. "You have no idea…Alex."

Despite several attempts to reignite the conversation, Colette returned her full attention to the file she had brought along. The logo with the four-pointed star stared back me. It must've been my imagination, but the bald eagle perched atop it looked to be facing the wrong way.

Although I hadn't eaten since breakfast, I didn't like the idea of filling my stomach with anything before the mission—Mox cola notwithstanding.

Despite the fact that I'd done little more than sit all day, I couldn't stop yawning. So I succumbed to the adrenaline hangover and slept my way across the country. Maybe further.

Wherever it was we landed was blanketed beneath a black sky filled with more stars than I would have thought possible. Apparently, Alexander the Late preferred remote locations when scoping out real estate for his lairs because the dry dirt and scrub grass provided few clues as to the geography.

But there could be no confusing our ultimate destination—a windowless, cube-shaped building that shared the same color as the drab landscape, or so the half-light of the quarter moon suggested.

Later I might marvel how the luxury jet had made a vertical landing precisely fifty yards from the tomb-like lair. At that moment, however, I found myself focusing on taking one breath after another and berating myself for being scared of an empty building.

I reminded myself that my evil twin was dead and my entourage, with Shadow Soldier 1 in front and Shadow Soldier 2 bringing up the rear, would keep me safe. I was in good hands.

Except it turned out I wasn't.

We were only a few feet from a somewhat-hidden door—the only interruption of the otherwise sandstone-textured metal—when two perfect circles on either side ejected themselves from the wall. I stared at the castoff coins for longer than I should have. Only when the sound of gunfire split the night did I notice the long cylinders protruding from where the lid-like circles had been.

Shadow Soldier 1 fell with a groan. Gunshots from behind indicated Shadow Soldier 2 was returning fire. I saw one of the two turrets explode as Colette grabbed my forearm and charged *toward* danger.

She chanted "shep" over and over as we ran up to a door that didn't open. Directly beside me, the remaining gun pivoted, adjusting its aim to account for Shadow

Soldier 2's evasive maneuvers. Sparks jumped from the metal above me, but none of the man's shots hit the target. A second later, Shadow Soldier 2 fell face down into the dirt.

Colette pounded on the door. "Open up, you flux-ridden piece of scat!"

I might have joined her in the show of pointless brute force, but I couldn't take my eyes off the big gun beside me. Was it built for close-range attacks? Or was the angle too acute for the thing to reach me?

I never discovered the answer because at that moment, the door slid open. Collette fell into a small alcove, pulling me inside with her. I scooted back until my butt hit a wall, which left less than ten feet between me and the grave outdoors.

"I don't understand," Colette said as she stared out into the night. "The security system never activated before. This door always opened for us..."

"Maybe the place finally figured out the boss is gone ...and it knows I'm an imposter."

She didn't answer, didn't even look at me. Spinning away from the open door, she walked up to the second one. The scanner beside the interior door might have been related to the ones I'd seen back in Chicago, except this box had a tiny hole in the center of the palm panel.

Colette drew her sidearm and extended her free hand toward me. "Up and at 'em, Alex. It's showtime."

Reflexively, I wrapped my fingers around hers and borrowed some of her momentum to stand. I almost suggested we make a beeline back to the jet, but even the thought of going deeper into the belly of the beast was somehow better than the prospect of facing the mounted machine gun outside.

"Maybe you should call for backup," I suggested. "Or

maybe the pilot could take out that last gun for us?"

Scorn dripped from her half-smile. "There is no pilot. It's all automated. Proxy Agents Wiggs and Bedge were the only ones who knew the exact coordinates of our destination. Even Jackson was kept in the dark…"

Turning to face me squarely, she said, "Our priority remains unchanged. You need to open this door."

"Shep," I swore, not knowing or caring what it really meant. The sooner I donated some blood, the sooner I could abandon this secret-agent nonsense and enjoy some good old-fashioned nightmares in my middle-class bed. "What do I have to do?"

Colette stepped aside so I could approach the panel. "Just press your palm against the sensor there. The needle will do the rest."

"Wonderful," I grumbled.

It took a shameful ten seconds for me to muster the courage to follow her simple instruction. I clenched my teeth and waited for the mechanical mosquito to do its thing. In spite of my best efforts, I gasped when the sharp pain pierced the center of my hand. Worse, I jerked it back so quickly I feared I'd have to do it all over again.

We shared a wordless glance as the tiny tube retreated back into the sensor.

"Do you think it…?

No need for me to finish the question. With the slightest hiss, the second door fell into a slot in the floor, revealing a room engulfed in absolute darkness. Whatever my feelings for the lovely Colette Lucier, no amount of macho bullshit was going to propel me into that abyss.

I was spared further humiliation, fortunately, when she said, "Wait here."

As soon as she stepped in front of the open door, a flash of light bloomed in the distance. I was about to ask Colette what it was when the woman slumped to the ground in front of me.

Gunfire.

With a silencer.

My beleaguered brain solved the mystery a moment too late. A second spark appeared, closer this time and illuminating the silhouette of a man my height. I'd have had to be a ninja to dodge the bullet. Or maybe a super-hero.

Since I was neither, the impact sent me down, crumpling beside the body of my beautiful companion.

When I opened my eyes, I realized I'd been wrong about two things.

First, it wasn't a bullet that had hit me, but some kind of tiny tranquilizer pellet.

Second, the gunman wasn't *about* my height. He was *exactly* my height.

For the second time that day, I found myself sitting alone in a room with a stranger, only this time the stranger wore my face—identical except for one thing.

"How'd you get that scar?" I asked, not because I was eager to confront my doppelganger or because I wanted to come off as cavalier. No, I was genuinely curious about the slight inaccuracy.

Death-defying Alexander Horn ran a hand through his slicked-back hair and smiled. "I was going to ask you the same thing, friend. They were so close to perfection, but they went and put your scar on the wrong side. Or did they want me to think I was looking in a mirror?"

My almost-twin and I sat in a luxuriously furnished room, the exact opposite of the industrial exterior and entryway I'd seen earlier. The fact that Other Me wore a deep purple robe and suede slippers might have been funny were it not for the revolver on his lap.

"*They* didn't put my scar anywhere," I insisted. "I got it when I was twelve…or maybe thirteen. I stupidly put my feet in my spokes while riding my bike. The thing flipped over, and I faceplanted on the street. Eight—"

"Stitches," he finished for me. "Exactly three days before our thirteenth birthday."

"I don't understand."

"Neither did I, not at first, but I think I'm on the verge of unraveling the riddle."

I leaned forward. For the World's Worst Human Being, he hadn't roughed me up nearly as much as Colette and her men. I wasn't even restrained, though his reaction to my sudden movement—a subtle positioning of his hand closer to the revolver—reminded me I was still at his mercy.

Or lack thereof.

"Did you kill Colette?" I asked weakly.

He waved away the question with a smoothness I myself never possessed. "Do you know who I am?"

"My clone. Or I'm yours. I haven't worked that part out yet."

Alexander Horn laughed, a mocking sound I hoped never to impersonate. "We're not clones. Desperate as the Domain United might have been to acquire my tech, they wouldn't have broken one of their most sacred laws. Even if they had, it would have taken longer to grow a viable clone, I imagine."

He stood and started pacing behind his throne of a chair. "And why bother giving you some inane backstory involving a bicycle?"

I waited for him to elaborate, to wave his magic wand of words so that this insane situation would finally start making sense. Instead, he said, "I also got my scar three days before my thirteenth birthday, only my accident involved a switchblade and my first murder."

He spun on a heel to face me. "Our father's name is Anthony. Our mother's is Samantha."

I scratched my head and found hair far less tidy than his. "So we're twins?"

"In a sense," he said. "How familiar are you with astronomical theories?"

"My degree is in information technology. The abstract stuff never made much sense to me," I admitted.

He nodded. "It was never my strong suit either, but I've compensated by making connections within the scientific community...particularly those unburdened by ethics. Anyway, one of my colleagues claimed to have made inroads while exploring the theory of the multi-verse."

"Meaning?"

Rolling his eyes, he said, "Meaning some people believe there are parallel universes...realities that are quite similar to one's own but with significant differences as well. A disparity in intellect. The placement of a scar. Apparently, the DU found merit in my friend's work and managed to pluck you from your world."

"I don't follow."

Only I did.

The notion was actually quite simple. We were the same person living in different worlds. Some mad scientist in this world opened a door between our dimensions and pulled clueless Alex Horn into this world for Mission: Incredible.

Given all I had seen since this morning, it made a lot of sense. I just didn't want to admit it.

"It hardly matters what you understand." My host

lowered himself back onto his pillow-full chair. "You share my face, my fingerprints, my DNA. That makes you a liability."

I remembered the revolver. Where had he stashed it?

"But it also makes you an *opportunity*."

"I don't follow." No lie this time.

"Come on…even someone as simple as you can wrap your mind around the benefits of having a body double. But that's thinking small. What would you say to being partners in crime?"

"I…I'm not exactly…evil," I told him.

The derisive laugh returned. "Is that what she told you…that I'm *evil*?"

"In so many words…and you *did* just kill some people."

Alexander Horn shrugged. "Soldiers die…but I'm guessing you're more concerned about a certain submarshall. I'm sure you found her absolutely irresistible…am I right?"

My scowl surely confirmed his suspicion.

"I merely tranq'd her" he said. "I am quite fond of Cole as well. She and I go way back. Though our history is complicated, I eagerly await our reunion."

"You two were…a couple?"

"Something like that." The criminal mastermind version of me pulled the gun from the fuzzy pocket of his robe. "When her team doesn't return, the DU will undoubtedly surmise I'm still alive, so I could use a few aces up my sleeve. I don't harbor any delusions that she and I will enjoy what we had before she learned of my ambitions, but I see no need to treat her poorly while she's a guest here."

"What about me?" I ventured.

He tapped the barrel of the revolver against his thigh.

"Yes, what *about* you? Can I call you Al?"

"Like the song," I snarked.

"What song?"

Oh man, a world without the hits of Paul Simon? And no melt-in-your-mouth M&M's? I'd never felt so home-sick. Finally, I managed to croak, "Alex."

"Works for me." Alexander spun the barrel of the gun dramatically. "What will it be, Alex? I am not 'evil,' but I *am* powerful, and I have a great vision for this world. What do you say you stick around and help me conquer mundanity?"

A thousand different responses came to mind—the boldest of them quickly melting on my tongue. What choice did I really have here? Alexander the Greater didn't have the means to send me back to blissfully sleepy Brookfield. Even if he did, he wouldn't let me slip through his fingers.

"I'm gonna miss my Earth," I said with a sigh.

And my cat, I silently added.

Alexander rose so quickly, I jerked in alarm. But the revolver fell safely to the ground, and when he reached for me, it was to put a firm hand on my shoulder. A show of solidarity despite our divided nature.

"Don't worry, Alex. It won't be forever." His smile widened. "Once Cole and you help me get my hands on whatever device allowed you to cross dimensions, we'll have a whole other world to conquer."

He laughed and added, "Imagine…a world that has never heard of Alexander Horn!"

I didn't know how to feel about that, how to feel about *any* of it. I couldn't fight him and couldn't run. At least I didn't faint this time.

Then again, maybe I could learn something from my devious double. Here was a man who didn't sit down to pee, and he had won the hand of Colette Lucier—albeit temporarily.

I'd always gone with the flow, avoided conflict, and worked only as hard as I'd had to. Maybe some good could come from navigating more tumultuous waters.

And, I had to admit, I looked pretty badass holding a gun.

Alexander returned to his chair, looked me up and down, and said, "The good news is all of my clothes will fit you, and I dress with style."

Before I could think of a suitable reply—*was* there a suitable reply?—a tabby jumped up onto his lap.

I smiled in spite of myself. "Horace?"

His grin matched my own. "You also have a cat named after the Egyptian god of light?"

The cat in question jumped from his lap to mine. The feel of his soft fur almost brought a tear to my eye. No need to tell my brother from another mother that *my* pet's name was a tribute to Horace Dodge, famed founder of a certain automobile company, not Horus.

If the laziest cat on my Earth could aspire to godhood here, certainly there was hope for an ordinary guy like me.

Reputation

To the untrained eye and unworldly mind, the small, blindfolded figure strapped to the chair looked to be little more than a defenseless child.

But Domacles Herronin knew better.

For one thing, his sentries had removed from the captive a half-dozen pouches containing odd ingredients, what wizards called "spell components." Then there was the intruder's staff, which now leaned against the far corner. Topped with an unidentified blue jewel, the accessory was more than an ordinary walking stick.

The confiscated conical hat—a wizardly cliché that predated the Wars of Sundering—clinched it.

"You're a midge," Domacles said, taking a seat on a stool across from the prisoner.

The fair-haired head turned back and forth, as though the futile motion might somehow help him see through the dark strip of cloth covering his eyes.

"No duh," the prisoner replied, "but I'm not just *any* midge."

Domacles stifled a sigh. A prevalent proverb throughout Continae insisted that dealing with a midge and enjoying a long, happy life were mutually exclusive. Truth be told, he had encountered only one midge during the three decades he had called the island province of

Capricon home.

That particular midge—a wrinkled, white-robe-wearing wizardess who claimed to be searching for the lost race of Altaerra—had been practically run out of town.

"Remove the blindfold," Domacles said with a wave of his hand.

The dark-skinned man in darker robes who stood behind the prisoner blanched. "But, sir, if he should identify you—"

Domacles interrupted Zicis with a laugh. "You said he came here with my name on his lips. Then you capture and bind him. Who else would he conclude I am?"

The other man scoffed. "With all due respect, sir, he's a *midge*. The gods only know what ridiculous thoughts bounce around those empty heads of theirs."

Domacles frowned. "I gave you an order, Master Vhemonte."

Biting his lower lip—and perhaps his tongue—the slim spell-caster unraveled the opaque ribbon. He then slammed the blindfold onto the table between Domacles and the prisoner. Although he said nothing, Zicis Vhemonte's expression said, "It's your funeral."

Domacles smiled, not only to put the prisoner at ease, but because he secretly relished the danger. "No risk, no reward" was a motto that had spurred him from a lowly sell-sword to the commander of his own mercenary band and beyond.

Having never matched wits with a midge before, the Renegade Leader welcomed this confrontation.

Besides, he was no stranger to the power of magic. He respected it, which was why he had welcomed Zicis into his company more than a year ago—and why Domacles hadn't perished during a clash with an enemy spell-caster two days ago.

"Thanks for getting that off," the midge said, blinking his big blue eyes against the lamplight. "My name is Noel. Are you the Hero? Your hair is really white, like an old person's, but you don't look like a grandpa. How old are you?"

Rather than run a hand self-consciously through his prematurely silvered hair, Domacles ignored the question and focused instead on the reference to his nickname, one he had invented himself, though rumors alleged his former clients and possibly even adversaries had bestowed the moniker upon him.

"Some call me Hero, yes. I am Domacles Herronin. How may I be of service to you, Master Noel?"

The midge squirmed in his chair, causing his bulky robe to bunch up by his neck. "You could start by untying me."

Still lurking behind Noel, Zicis scowled. Domacles nearly acquiesced, if only to watch the man sweat. But Domacles hadn't earned the love of his men by aggravating them needlessly, and recent setbacks had tested everyone's resolve.

Risktaker though he was, Domacles was not a reckless man.

"Please forgive the ill treatment, but you must understand our need for caution," Domacles began. "The midge are renowned for their magical prowess. Indeed, your people number among the most powerful wizards in all the world. Until we get to know you better, I am afraid you must endure a little discomfort…for *our* safety."

Noel's face bunched up in confusion. Perhaps the little man was trying to decide whether he should feel honored or offended by his continued captivity.

Domacles smiled. While he had earned his silver-white hair at a young age, he had possessed a silver tongue even longer.

"I guess it's all right," Noel said. "Because we're gonna be really good friends soon. I can be a big help *because* of my magic. I'm a black-robe…well, my actual robe is blue, but I get my spells from Vhestaz, the Goddess of Black Magic. She's not evil, though…not really. She's just really tough, which is why I chose her. Because I'm a *warrior*. I once made a fireball so big that it…well, let's just say that mean ol' giant wouldn't have been able to sit down for a month…if he hadn't died. What I'm trying to say is black-robes are really, really good at battle magic."

Zicis sneered. "We know what a black-robe is, you simpleton. *I* am one."

Noel rolled his eyes and muttered, "Barely."

As Zicis fumed, Domacles coughed to cover his laugh. "Indeed, Master Vhemonte has served me well in matters arcane since before the Renegade War began. What makes you think my band needs another spell-caster?"

And why would a midge want to join the rebellion? he wondered.

Noel's grin stretched from one hairless cheek to the other. "Like I said earlier, I'm not just any midge. I'm a hero too…maybe the greatest midge hero since Keelah the Champion. I recently saved an entire world, ya know. You *need* me."

Zicis' laugh overflowed with scorn. "We need a midge like we need more lice in the barracks."

Domacles crossed his arms. "Mind your manners, Master Vhemonte, or you will be asked to leave."

Noel stuck out his tongue but couldn't turn enough in his chair for the other wizard to see it.

Folding his hands and leaning forward, Domacles said, "You will have to forgive me, Noel, but I had not heard

Altaerra owed its ongoing existence to a midge savior. That sounds like quite a story."

Noel's smile faded a little. "Actually, it wasn't Altaerra. It was a *different* world. The gods sent me and a few other heroes to this other world, where we had to fight four big, scary monsters, travel back in time to fight them all over again, and then battle this freaky gargoyle-looking thing that wanted to ruin that realm forever."

Zicis threw up his hands. "So this is how we are to spend our evening? Listening to a small man spin tall tales?"

"I'm not lying!" Noel snapped.

"I know a spell that can pry truth from the tongue," Zicis returned, "though I doubt it would work on a mind as addled as yours."

The midge pressed his feet against the floor, tipping his chair back. Zicis was forced to catch it or take the brunt with his belly. Now looking down at the prisoner, Zicis couldn't miss a second appearance from the tongue in question. Zicis pushed the chair back to the floor and then raised a hand to strike Noel.

"Enough!" Domacles shouted, causing both mages to flinch. "You are dismissed, Master Vhemonte."

Zicis' jaw dropped. "But—"

"Have you warded this room against magic?" Domacles asked.

"Of course, but—"

"Then I bid you good night."

Zicis looked like he was going to argue. Domacles had been told his gray eyes could pierce as strongly as the steel they resembled. He leveled a perfectly lethal stare at the wizard. Zicis gulped, gave a slight blow, and backed out of the room.

Returning his gaze to Noel, Domacles found an abashed expression clouding the midge's face. He had to remind himself that he had not scolded an innocent child, but rather challenged an enemy who could end up being a greater threat than the combined forces of the Knights of Superius.

Domacles sat up straighter. "I apologize, again, for Master Vhemonte's behavior. He was bested by a red-robe not two days ago, and I believe that failure yet chafes him."

"I wasn't lying," Noel mumbled, not looking Domacles in the eye.

In that moment, Domacles could forgive every warrior who had ever underestimated a midge. It was all too easy to sympathize with the childlike race who not only looked, but also acted like human children.

Children who could cook a giant with a few choice words…

Perhaps Zicis had been right about one thing: a lie-detecting spell wouldn't have worked on Noel. The midge seemed to genuinely believe his own outlandish story.

Not that Domacles needed to verify the details of his history. No, the Renegade Leader was far more interested in Noel's present—and future.

"Why have you sought me out, Master Noel?"

The midge took a deep breath. "When I came back to Altaerra, I couldn't find Zack or Klye or Earl…those were the other heroes I mentioned…so I went to Therrat to talk with my good friend Avuru. He's a midge who has also spent a lot of time around humans because he runs a store…and it's a store that sells magical stuff, though that's a secret, so please don't tell anyone…and I told him all about how I saved that *other* world and how I wanted to keep being a hero in *this* world, except nothing exciting ever happens in Ristidae…not since the Ogrebasher War anyway…"

Noel took another big breath. "So then Avuru tells me about this *new* war that's going on in the west. Knights versus Renegades. The Knights fight for the Kings of Continae, who want to unite the world in peace. Even Pickelo South, the midge homeland, signed the Scroll of Alliance! So I thought, 'Well, I'd better help the Knights because those Renegades are gonna mess it all up for everyone."

When Domacles didn't say anything after several seconds, Noel added, "And that's why I want to fight in the Renegade War."

Domacles suddenly wished he hadn't sent Zicis away—at least not before ordering the wizard to fetch a bottle of wine. Without ever casting a spell, the midge had conjured up a fair measure of discomfort in the form of Domacles' stiff shoulders and a hint of a headache blooming at the back of his skull.

Nonetheless, Domacles smiled. "Master Noel, I am afraid I have been remiss in my duties as a host. Please allow me to bring us some wine so that we do not become parched during our fine conversation."

As he passed the midge, Noel asked, "Do you have any elf water?"

Domacles resisted the urge to grimace. Elf water had to be the sweetest white wine in all the world. He supposed he shouldn't have been surprised to learn his childlike prisoner preferred what amounted to liquid confection, though Domacles would have sooner imbibed bloodwine from the Deathlands than drink elf water.

"I shall see what I can find," he said over his shoulder.

No sooner did he close the door than a slim figure separated from the shadows in the hall. Even after years fighting beside the lithe woman on the battlefield,

Domacles marveled at Sair's grace—a carryover from her former life as a *sai-mori* assassin.

"You heard all he said?" Domacles asked.

Sair nodded, her dark eyes glinting in the dim light of the corridor.

He knew that if he told her to walk into the room and slit the midge's throat, she would do so without hesitation. She had risked her life for him more times than he could count. But while he believed she loved him, even her loyalty had its limits.

Which was why the order he wanted to give her was currently stuck in his throat.

Sair raised a thin eyebrow and asked, "Has he really come here to fight Renegades? Are we to lose this base too?"

Domacles looked away. Staring at the closed door, he imagined the cryptic little man on the other side. Their hideout was among Capricon's best-kept secret, one that had recently saved their lives after a swift retreat from North Port.

If the Knights had sent Noel as a diversion—or, worse, the vanguard—while Sir Magmund's troops surrounded their base…

Domacles shook his head. "We are not leaving yet. I do not believe the Knights sent him."

"Because he is a mage?" Sair asked. "I seem to recall an Ahuli wizard fighting alongside the Knights of Fort Miloásterôn."

"Not because he is a mage, but because he is a *midge*," Domacles clarified. "No Knight of Superius would choose so unpredictable, so *undependable* an ally."

He glanced over at Sair. It was impossible to tell whether the woman agreed with him. She might as well have been wearing a porcelain mask for how little her expression changed from moment to moment. The same held true on the battlefield. And in the bedroom.

"What do you want me to do?" Sair asked.

Domacles cleared his throat and willed himself not to blush. "Fetch some wine for the prisoner and me."

Up went the eyebrow again—along with a blade he hadn't seen earlier. She pressed the cold blade against his throat as she spoke.

"Is this why I forsook honorable Clan Whisperstrike, to play barmaid for a would-be warlord?"

Domacles rolled his eyes. "If half your tales are true, you have played worse roles while navigating the intrigues of Huiyah. Delivering the wine gives you an excuse to join us. You will then stay and assist with the interrogation."

As suddenly as the knife appeared, it was gone. Sair bowed deeply. "Your wish is my command, Lord Herronin."

He was tempted to swat her backside as she walked away but didn't push his luck. Though he knew Sair Relice better than any man alive or dead, he was ever one misstep away from leaving the former to join the latter.

Shaking away such morbid thoughts, Domacles reentered the room to find Noel sitting cross-legged on the table.

Not in his chair.

Not tied up.

The midge sat facing away from him. Domacles reached for the broadsword strapped to his back but didn't draw the weapon. Noel could have reclaimed his staff and other magical accoutrements, kicked open the door, and torched him. A quick glance in the corner confirmed that the jewel-topped rod remained where Zicis had placed it.

Hands at his side—the fingers of his left hand lingering

an inch from his dagger—Domacles said, "Master Noel?"

The midge turned around to let his feet dangle over the side of the table.

Light from the lamp flashed across the small knife in his hand.

"Oh, hi."

Domacles forced a smile. "You have left your seat."

Noel glanced at the chair. "Yeah. The ropes were kinda itchy. I didn't think you'd care if I disintegrated them because we're friends now. That's why you went to get us something to drink, right?"

Domacles might have asked how Noel had performed a spell while tied up in a supposedly warded room, but he had a more pressing question on his mind.

"And what of the knife?"

Noel looked down at the blade as though noticing it for the first time and said, "Spider."

"You named your knife Spider?"

Noel laughed loudly and hopped down from the table. Domacles took a step back in spite of himself. The midge retrieved something from the table and held it out to Domacles in his cupped hands.

It was a dead arachnid.

"Spider legs come in handy when you want to cast sticky spells," he explained. "I once climbed onto the ceiling so I could scare my buddy Plean. He's kinda paranoid to begin with. Anyway, I dispelled the enchantment right when he was beneath me and made this loud *RAWR*ing sound as I fell on him. Plean was so surprised! He stabbed me twice with his magical knives before he realized it was me!"

Domacles, who had always prided himself on knowing the right thing to say, was speechless.

Noel gingerly put the dead spider back on the table.

"I'm sorry. Maybe Master Vee-whatever should get the legs, since he's been here longer."

Domacles laughed. Whether he was laughing at himself, the midge, or the situation, he did not know. As he circled the table and reclaimed his chair, he said, "You can keep the spider, Master Noel. Consider it a gift."

By the time Noel deposited the tiny corpse into one of his pouches and sheathed his small blade, Sair was knocking on the door. She then entered carrying a tray. Domacles thought the midge lucky indeed that she hadn't walked in while Noel was waving his weapon around.

Perhaps Noel was indeed blessed by the gods.

Sair didn't have to raise an eyebrow as she set the contents of the tray—a pair of stemless glasses and a bottle of Shadrach Red—onto the table. The message she silently sent when their eyes met told Domacles that she believed he had misjudged the situation and that she was ready to rectify his error at a moment's notice.

Domacles didn't know what weapons she had smuggled into the interrogation room. It hardly mattered. Sair herself was a weapon.

Noel swept some ash from his seat before sitting down. He smiled at Sair and said, "Hi, I'm Noel. Who are you?"

Sair gave a slight bow but said nothing in reply.

"Master Noel." Domacles poured the red-violet liquid into two cups. "Earlier you used the phrase 'Knights versus Renegades.' To which faction do you believe I belong?"

Noel made a strange face. Domacles couldn't decide if his question or the sour contents of the glass was responsible. Then the midge laughed.

"Is this some kind of test?" he asked.

Domacles smiled. "Indulge me. Please."

With a carefree shrug, Noel replied, "All right. You

have a huge sword strapped to your back. You wear shiny metal armor. That other mage called you "sir" before, and when you talk, you don't say 'don't.' You say 'do not,' just like the Knights of Superius up in Continae. Plus they call you *the Hero*!

"So you're obviously an important Knight!"

It took all of Domacles' discipline not to guffaw at the absurd notion. While Domacles had long ago adopted a courtly style and chivalrous decoration, he had done so ironically. There was nothing noble about Domacles Herronin, who fought for coin and battled for glory. The little twit must have overheard someone refer to him as "the Hero" and filled in the blanks incorrectly.

He could have told Noel the truth, explaining that "Hero" was a derivation of his surname and that while his father had been a Knight of Eaglehand in Glenning, his bastard son had no such aspirations. He might have even explained that Noel had somehow managed to stumble upon a most-wanted enemy of any Knight pledged to defend the fledgling Alliance of Nations.

But while Domacles Herronin flirted with danger, he did not court death. The midge's confusion currently served as a shield, and he would not discard that advantage.

"That's why I wanted to join your group," Noel said after another sip of his wine. "No elf water, huh? Anyway, it's really boring just wandering around after you've been an important hero in another world. I want to make a difference and stop the bad guys. Because that's what the gods want me to do."

Domacles knew he should be scheming for a way to send Noel on his way without raising suspicion—or hurting the capricious creature's feelings—but he couldn't resist asking, "Why do you think the gods have sent you to Capricon?"

Noel beamed. "You want to hear the rest of my story? Wow. Usually, humans don't believe anything I say and tell me to go away. Then again, you're a *hero*, one of the good guys. Well, after I chatted with Avuru…you remember Avuru, right? The midge who runs a mageware shop in Therrat that you promised not to tell anyone about?"

Domacles gave a slight nod.

"After I chatted with Avuru, I went to Superius because that's where the king who *invented* the Alliance of Nations lives. I stopped at the first castle I found, but it wasn't the royal palace or anything. It was called Fort Something-or-other…like Fort Strength but fancier. The Knights wouldn't let me in, not even after I told them that I wanted to help them kick the Renegades' butts."

Domacles raised his glass in mock toast. He would've paid a hundred suns to see the looks on those Knights' faces as a midge walked up to their gates.

"But then one of the warriors came out, and we had a nice long chat," Noel continued. "At first I didn't think he liked me very much, but after I told him all about how I saved that other world and how even black magic can do good things if the spell-caster is a good guy, like me, he must've warmed up to me because he told me exactly how I could be a big help to the war effort."

Domacles reached for his glass but did not drink.

"He told me that there was another hero…*the* Hero… down in Capricon. The Knight said the Hero is a really brave guy who has been pushing the boundaries of the rebellion. He told me I should come to the island and find Domacles Herronin because that would make a big difference in the war."

Domacles nearly dropped his glass. If he had heard this part of Noel's account from the start, he might have dismissed it as a tall tale. The whole thing seemed too preposterous to contain any truth.

Yet the only lie Domacles could detect was the one which that Knight of Superius had told the gullible midge.

Suddenly, Domacles heard a sound he had never heard before—a high-pitched giggle over his left shoulder. He turned, astonished, to find Sair covering her mouth with her hands.

"Seriously?" he said to her.

"I'm sorry, sir, but—" She fought off another wave of laughter. When she was able to compose herself once more, she said, "In all of my days skulking about Huiyah, engaging in subterfuge for sly feudal lords jockeying for position, I have never encountered so devious a plot. We have gravely misjudged our enemies."

Domacles couldn't deny that sending an unwitting agent of chaos into the Renegades' ranks was as underhanded a maneuver as he could conceive.

If Noel discovered Domacles and his company were, in fact, rebels, he would wreak untold havoc upon the troupe. Which hamstrung Domacles' counterattack on North Port in the short term and possibly sidelined his efforts indefinitely for fear of Noel betraying his location —intentionally or unintentionally.

And if the midge perished while fighting the rebels, the Knights would likely see it as a double win.

"Fort Fortitude!"

Domacles jumped at Noel's exclamation.

"That's the name of the fort near the Ristidae border," Noel explained. "It's kind of a silly name if you think about it. It's like you're repeating yourself…Fort Fort…"

Another giggle escaped from the deadly assassin beside Domacles.

The Renegade Leader wished he could share his

companion's mirth. The bitter taste in his mouth had nothing to do with this particular vintage from the Oaken Kingdom.

The Knights of Fort Miloásterôn had outmaneuvered him on the battlefield mere days ago. With that sting still fresh, the joke played upon him by the Knights of Fort Fortitude felt like salt in the wound.

Domacles Herronin was nobody's dupe.

Wiping the purple stain from his lips, Noel asked, "So how many Renegade Leaders are there in Capricon anyway?"

Rather than answer, Domacles studied the midge before him. The easiest way out of this snare was to kill Noel. It was also the smart play. As powerful a mage as Noel surely was—possessing both the incantations and whit to find the Renegades' hidden base of operations—Domacles knew Sair could sever the little man's windpipe before he squeaked out a single syllable of a spell.

Yet Noel was not his enemy. The Knights were. And the best way to get back at them was to beat them at their own dirty game.

Domacles refilled their glasses. "Master Noel, I am honored and humbled to make your acquaintance. By adding your magic to my forces, I do not doubt we could rid this region of those nefarious rebels. However, I know of someone who is in more need of your assistance."

"Oh really?"

For the next few minutes, Domacles shared everything he had learned about a fresh-faced Knight of Superius bound for a derelict fortress to the southeast. A trusted friend and Renegade Leader from Continae had warned him of the new troops being sent to the island. Now Domacles passed along what he knew of the young man who had surely reached Fort Faith by now—a warrior with his own nickname.

"Do you really think Commander Colt needs my help?" Noel asked.

"Indeed," Domacles was quick to reply. "Rumor has it that a new Renegade Leader has arrived in Capricon and is hells-bent on harassing the Knights at Fort Faith. He has no spell-caster in his ranks and could certainly benefit from a bona fide hero at his side."

Noel puffed out his chest a little as he sat up straighter in his chair. "I thought I came to fight beside a fellow hero, but maybe it's better if I teach somebody *else* how to be a hero."

Leaning forward to rest a hand on the midge's shoulder, Domacles said, "You are wise beyond your years, Master Noel."

"So are you...though I still don't know how old you are. All that white hair but no wrinkles!"

When Sair escorted the midge from the room, insisting that she draw Noel a map to Fort Faith and give him a proper sendoff, Domacles lingered in the small room.

After downing the contents of his glass, he reached for the bottle and brought it up to his lips.

"If the gods truly sent you to Capricon, I can think of no worthier cause for you, Master Noel," he said, raising the almost-empty bottle in the air.

"And no better way to turn the Knights' secret weapon against them!"

Captive

I must have been asleep because I was just talking to my mother, who died in 2038.

I'm in bed, a somewhat inclined apparatus that's too soft against my lower back and too hard behind my head. I reach for the bleach-white pillow by my hip. A pinch of pain by my hand stops me.

The long tube extending from my wrist connects to what might be an IV—a beyond-space-age pod that hovers at my bedside.

Soundlessly, the drone floats closer to me, giving me more slack. Forgetting the pillow and my stiff neck, I stare at its shiny shell, bluer than the summer sky over the Caspian.

It's in this moment I realize this is not my bed and not my home. The bright, blank walls have been stripped of any personalization, lacking even the obligatory decorations hotel rooms provide. Not even a window, though the opaque screen encompassing the narrow wall at the foot of my bed resembles one in size and shape.

Someone has gone to a lot of trouble to emulate a hospital room, but I'm not buying it. Even after getting grazed by a bullet in the six-week war of 2020, I've never needed overnight care in a medical facility. We Cafarova women are renowned for our durability, dating back to my grandmother, who was shot twice in Baku, once when trying to repel the Soviet invaders and again when fighting beside her former enemies against the Nazis.

More importantly, I haven't seen combat in years. I'm retired. Or about to be.

So why the ruse?

In defiance of my crescendoing heartbeat, I take a series of deep, soothing breaths. The temptation to yank the tube from my veins is strong, but that will surely alert somebody. I'm not ready to confront my captor—not until I understand who is holding me and why.

I strain to remember where I was before I slept. My mother was there, hugging me. No, that's just a remnant of a dream, an almost-memory of me displaying my new uniform to the woman who had survived two coups during her service.

My thoughts are cloudy, compelling me to close my eyes and reunite with my ana. I blame it on whatever drug my foes have coursing through me.

If the Armenians have made me their prisoner, I can't fathom why. Yes, I have a command, but I am of no value to them as a hostage. Neither do I know anything that will give them a greater advantage in our ongoing contest for Nagorno-Karabakh.

Or has Russia returned for our oil?

Maybe Iran has decided to widen its reach in the Muslim world?

Some part of my mind insists I have left the East, though whether the idea was suggested by my state-of-the-art prison cell or a phantom memory of arriving in the United States by jet, I can't say.

"*Sikim*."

No sooner has the curse left my chapped lips than a voice emits from nowhere and everywhere:

"Good morning, Ms. Cafarova. I hope you had a good rest."

Female. English with an American accent. The tone was friendly, perhaps youthful.

I stay quiet. I want to close my eyes to feign sleep but can't risk falling beneath the waves of pharmaceutical lethargy. It's all I can do to stay present. My memories are hundreds of puzzle pieces, facedown and scattered across an uneven surface. I try to find the protocol for prisoners of war, but I can't recall my training.

"Is there anything I can get you?" the invisible lady asks.

English has never come easily to me, so I'm surprised how quickly a sarcastic response forms in my mind. I swallow it.

"Why am I being held here?" My voice sounds weak and rusty.

"You were relocated to Unit B on 6-15-2053 to ensure your safety while you recover."

"How generous of you." I glare at the suspended IV drone. I wrap my fingers around the thin, transparent tube. "I demand you release me!"

"My apologies, Ms. Cafarova, but it's important that you remain in bed and heal. Would you care for some music? Or for me to play a stream for you?"

I couldn't care less about background noise, ambient or otherwise. Is this some new tactic? If so, it's an obvious ploy to make me feel comfortable and off-guard.

It won't work.

"Are you hungry?" the disembodied voice asks.

I am not, though I can't remember the last time I ate. My grandmother's *piti* comes to mind. I'd swear I had some yesterday. Impossible, unless I prepared the soup myself—an unlikely prospect for a deployed soldier. Still,

I see a kitchen with an old woman who looks a little like my aunt or how I myself might appear in my late retirement. The children, with their round faces and wide noses, look like Carafova stock—strangers both.

"Who are those kids?" I ask myself.

"I can show you pictures of your kids," my captor volunteers. "Just a moment, and I'll bring up the display."

"I don't have any kids, you *gijdillax*!"

Surely this is psychological warfare. Stubborn and forthright, I've never had much luck with men. Anyway, my chances of conceiving were compromised by a childhood ailment.

How my enemy knows this remains an agonizing mystery.

I tighten my grip on the IV feed but stop short of tugging because a series of images appear on the wall-screen before me. I see myself, but I'm much older than I should be. Age-advancing software, surely. But the young faces of a boy and girl—and the man behind them, presumably their fictional father—mimic false memories that fill in before and after the still frames.

Have I seen these pictures before? Did my captors go to the trouble of manufacturing the traditional Azerbaijani wedding ceremony, or did my beleaguered brain engineer the highlights reel I'm now imagining?

Even my battalion tattoo is faded in the on-screen images.

When the wrinkled black-and-white photo of my grandmother in Soviet garb appears, I cry out in fury and give the drug line a sudden pull. The pusher drone draws nearer, but it's lazy pace cannot compensate for my speed. Three droplets of blood spray the machine, then slide down its shiny blue carapace.

"Ms. Carafova, you have become disconnected from

your LifeLine unit. Assistance will arrive shortly."

"That's Capt. Carafova, you smug *sikim*!"

There's no telling how long it will take my captors to arrive. I swing my legs over the side of my bed. Clenching my teeth against a sharp pain in my hip, I slowly lower my feet to the floor.

Immediately I fall—not because of the anticipated lightheadedness from whatever drugs still swim through my system, but from an inferno of pain that saps all strength from my left leg.

My shoulder clips the side of the bed on the way down. I manage to get an arm out to brace myself, preventing a head injury. Maybe I'm already concussed. That would explain a lot.

But there isn't time to ponder how I got here and why the withered leg beneath my robe is wrapped in a foamy bandage.

I must rise.

I make an attempt and almost pass out from the pain. A weapon then. Yes, if I can find some means to defend myself, I might be able to take out one of my captors before they realize what's happening.

Half lying, half sitting, I reach into the top of my robe, hoping to find a bra with an underwire that can be fashioned into a gouging tool. Instead I find a pair of breasts that are too long and loose to belong to a thirty-year-old athlete.

The hated hovering bot rounds the edge of the bed, lowers itself to my level, and watches me eyelessly.

I want to kick the thing, but I know another wave of pain will rob me of what little senses I have left. Whoever has imprisoned me—some terrorist cell or the CIA—has rendered me completely helpless. I long to return to my mother's embrace.

My heavy eyelids separate when a door I couldn't discern from the wall a second ago opens. The woman is larger and older and darker than how I imagined the taunting voice from earlier. When she speaks, I know she is someone else.

"Oh, Maryam. We're gonna have to use the restraints now, I sup—no, don't try to stand, dear. I'll get you reconnected to your LifeLine. It'll help you sleep."

"No!" I lash out at the woman in white.

She easily catches my sluggish punch. My shout turns into a moan, though not from the pain. No, for the first time since waking in this foreign prison, I get a really good look at my arm. Dark veins snake along the underside, but that's not nearly as unnerving as the battalion of furrows occupying my once-beautiful olive skin.

"What have you done to me?" I demand.

The woman frowns, not meeting my eyes. I curse at her in my native tongue, mixing in a few English swears and even a few Russian insults I inherited from my father. She ignores me as I struggle against her hold, unable to stop her from reattaching me to the drone.

A cold sensation fills my forearm and spreads slowly up my shoulder. The dark-skinned woman in the bright uniform pats my hand. "Oh, Maryam. Your kids are so worried about you."

"But I don't have…any…"

I trail off. Confusion, anger, and guilt—these free-floating feelings and more roll in with the tranquilizer haze. For an instant, those familiar strangers from the screen gain names: my beloved Nazim, sweet Samir, and Madina, who can beat a boy twice her size in a scuffle.

They are young, then older, adults with children of their own.

I close my eyes. My long-dead mother refills my soup

bowl, wipes her hands on her apron, and kisses me on the top of my head.

"Rest, my dear. All will be well."

And whether those words are from my ana or the nurse, I must believe them.

The Fix

I noticed her tits first. The low-cut dress exposed more of the shapely pair than it hid. But it was the giant gemstone perched in her cleavage, sparkling despite the dubious lighting of the club, that made my eyes linger.

Sipping my bourbon at a high table, I took a moment to appreciate the alluring display. When I finally glanced higher, I found Blondie scanning the bar area, looking for a friend. Or maybe a friendly stranger.

Her face was passably pretty. Good. That always made it easier.

As she walked up to the bar, I watched the sheer white material caress her curves. The dress looked expensive. So did the diamonds dangling from her ears. Overdressed, despite the skimpy gown.

If she wasn't meeting someone, I'd make sure she met me.

"Looks like you're running on empty, darlin'."

I stifled a frown and turned to the owner of the drawl. White. Old. But not too old. His watch was worth a grand easy.

"Want me to fill 'er up?" he asked, his gaze migrating south from mine.

I sat up straighter to put my physique at its best vantage. Probably should've popped my top button open earlier, but how was I to know ol' nicotine breath was prowling my blind spot?

I emptied my glass. "Knob Creek, no ice."

It wasn't what I had been drinking, but I often ordered that vaguely phallic brand when men asked. The lips beneath his white-streaked mustache curled upward.

His eyes didn't smile though. They burned with an appetite that would grow the more he drank. I tried to remember if I'd seen Tex during my thirty-some minutes of surveying the place from my corner seat. No luck.

"My pleasure, darlin'."

He couldn't've been too drunk because he picked up my empty glass with a steady, manicured hand. His widening smile formed furrows around those hungry eyes.

While Tex tried to get the attention of a server, I glanced back at the bar, where Blondie laughed with a middle-class woman whose hand rested possessively on the thigh of the guy next to her. The stool on the other side of Blondie was empty.

There was still time to move in.

Before I could come up with a strategy to extricate myself from the aging cowboy, a woman came to take our order. Tex took great pains to show the healthy contents of his wallet as he plucked a hundred from inside.

OK then.

I turned in toward Tex. Putting Blondie out of my sightline and out of mind. Giving my new mark my undivided attention.

"Tom Collins for me and Knob Creek for the lady here." After she left, he added, "You *are* a lady, aren't you?"

No way to know if he was alluding to my gender or general decency, so I stalled. "Are you looking for a lady?"

His chuckle sent another wave of smoke-reek into my nostrils. "I'm here on business, and *my* lady is at home. What I'm lookin' for is some fun."

I wondered why he'd bother hiding his wedding ring if he wasn't shy about infidelity. Maybe it was in his pocket. I'd find out soon enough. Men were easier to manipulate than women. More physical than emotional.

Make him feel important. Stroke his ego. And maybe something else.

"Fun just happens to be my middle name," I replied with a wink.

"Yeah? An' what's your first?"

"Nic."

He scoffed. "You sure don't make it easy for a guy. Are you a chick pretendin' to be a dude or a dude posin' as a chick?"

No getting around the question this time. Tex wanted to know what he'd find between my legs.

Or did he? The man was obviously looking for someone very different from the presumably plump housewife he'd left south of the Mason-Dixon. I was young, dark-skinned, androgynous. He liked what he saw.

Tex craved adventure, and I'd give him one.

Just not the way he wanted.

"You'll just have to find out," I purred.

He barked a laugh, dropped a hand to my thigh, and squeezed. I waited for him to home in on my crotch, but the Southern adulterer was content to let the mystery linger. I'd made the right call.

Shifting in my seat, I shot a glance back at Sparkle Tits. The couple beside her wasn't paying her any attention anymore. Blondie's elbows were up on the bar, her head in her hands. The way her shoulders shook suggested sobbing.

Sloppy drunks had their own pros and cons. Blondie needed comforting. A shoulder to cry on. A compassionate stranger who could make her feel loved. Far more work than a handjob.

But damn it all, why'd Tex have to be a smoker?

While waiting for our drinks, we made small talk. He was in town for a conference on innovation. He wasn't a tech guy himself, but he bankrolled engineers, scientists, and "the like." I feigned interest as he waxed altruistic about making the world better one advancement at a time.

"And maybe someday the rest of us'll be able to afford a sexbot," I joked during the silence between nearly identical songs.

His artificially white teeth caught a glint of light from the dancefloor. "And why is it, with all the breakthroughs in AI and the wide-sweepin' applications, everybody gets stuck on the fucking?"

"Sex sells?" I said with a shrug.

"Sex *innovates*," he corrected. "From steering mainstream media formats to best practices in e-commerce, the sex industry has always been a pioneer of new tech. VR would've died without porn. Which probably means nobody will have a helper 'bot in their home until the sex dolls work out all the kinks."

"So to speak."

He raised his glass, and we clinked. I pretended to spill a little and laughed it off. I wasn't even buzzed, thanks to an intentionally high tolerance level. But the quicker he thought I was tipsy, the sooner we could get on with it.

Tex dabbed at my shirt with a cocktail napkin. Not to be a gentleman. He was doing some pioneering himself. Searching for pecs or tits, though only he knew which he was hoping to find.

"Stuff goes straight to my head," I said. "We should go

somewhere more…quiet. Where are you staying?"

He hesitated. Maybe sensing danger on a primal level. Or maybe he was a first-time cheater, and the reality of the situation was catching up to him. Either way, I had to take matters into my own hands to ensure a profitable night.

Cupping the front of his pants, applying slight pressure, I slurred, "Well, there's no doubt *you're* a man."

Lust overcame whatever reservations he had. We pounded our drinks, and I followed him from the table. Humans were easy to hack. Too damn easy.

Funny thing was I used to think there was something wrong with me, something *broken*. It wasn't that the milk of human kindness had gone sour so much as it had evaporated completely. Or had never been poured into me to start with.

But it was never a defect. Quite the opposite. The real crime was *pretending* to care. Having shed my vestigial conscience, I had evolved.

On our way past the bar, a broad-shouldered man in an expensive suit bumped past me. I should've let it go. Instead I stopped and turned. He made a beeline to the empty seat next to Blondie and grabbed her wrist roughly.

I glanced at Tex, halfway to the exit and oblivious to the fact I wasn't right behind him. Back at the bar, Blondie tried to wrench free of the guy's grasp. Whatever she shouted at him was swallowed up by the thundering bass beat.

Tex held open the door, but I wasn't there to accept his courtesy. He waved. I looked away, walked away—like a fool—toward Blondie and her beau.

"—never go back there with you," she was yelling. "You're just…just…*using* me!"

The guy scoffed. "Don't be ridiculous."

"You *made* me ridiculous!"

Blondie tried to slap him, but her palm halted a couple inches from his cheek. The diamond necklace swung wildly at the sudden stop. The stone sure looked real—realer than her chest at any rate.

She made a noise that was part shout, part scream. The man and I both flinched.

He took a step back, but his hand was still wrapped around her wrist. "Don't make a scene, Bettie."

"Easy there," I said, inserting myself between them. "Looks like the lady isn't interested in your company tonight."

His brow crinkled in confusion. Like I was speaking Klingon at a Star Wars convention. He probably wasn't used to having his authority questioned. Leastwise from his trophy wife here.

No, not married. Neither of them wore a ring.

The man glared at me. "She's…look, this isn't what it looks like. Just mind your own business, and—"

"What's the holdup, Nic?" Tex asked, coming up behind me.

"Just making sure my friend Bettie here is safe," I replied, never taking my eyes off her unwelcome companion.

Tex snorted. "She looks like an escort. Wait, are *you* an escort?"

I spun around. The cigarette stench of his accusation lingered. That, combined with the look of disgust in the hypocrite's eyes, was simply too much.

"Fuck you, old man."

Tex stormed off, but not before something dangerous swept across his face. Over his shoulder, he called me a bitch. I didn't know if he'd decided I was a female after all or if that's what he called everyone who crossed him.

I didn't care.

I had another alpha male to contend with.

Frowning, the man tugged Bettie's arm. She stumbled off of her bar stool, moaning in a way most folks would have called pitiable but which I found pitiful. The whole damsel-in-distress scenario made me sigh. But in for a penny, in for a pound.

It wasn't that I hated violence on principle. I just reserved it for last resorts. Like the pistol hidden by my ankle. Some people called them fuck-me boots. I liked to think of them as fuck-*you* boots.

If I was going to be Bettie's hero, I had to play the part.

"You don't own her," I said evenly.

"Actually, I do."

I sucker punched the bastard so hard I could've gotten his dental records from my knuckles.

He crumpled to the ground. Must've knocked him out cold because he didn't move. Beside me, Blondie could've been laughing or crying. With those bulging blue eyes of hers and the ugly sounds pouring from her throat, it was impossible to tell.

"Hey now!" The bartender—a young thing with muscles more for decoration than application—scowled at me. "Take her and get out before I call the cops."

I rolled my eyes. "Things might not've gotten out of hand if you hadn't overserved her."

The bartender threw his hands up. "She ordered water!"

"Come on," I said to Bettie.

She didn't resist as I led her through the crowd of gawkers. Her hand was soft and hot. And strong. I wouldn't have minded seeing *her* slug that guy. But she couldn't even bring herself to slap him. Not the violent type.

Good.

When we got outside, I didn't let go of her hand. "I should make sure you get home safely."

Bettie's eyes widened. They were shiny with unspent tears. "You don't understand! I ran away, and I can't go back! Please don't make me!"

"OK, OK, relax."

Her hand went limp in mine. I reluctantly released it.

"You don't have to go home, Bettie, but is there someplace else you can go?"

"Can I go home with you?"

I couldn't fight the frown. I never took anybody back to my place, least of all marks. It was one thing for a hungover victim to tell the police they had been conned by someone named Nic. Even if they described me to a sketch artist, it wouldn't be enough to track me down.

I didn't have a record, and I didn't have a record because I was too smart to take pathetic rich ladies home with me.

"Look…it's Bettie, right?" She nodded. "My place is a mess, but I can get you to a hotel, and—"

"I don't have any money."

I almost grabbed the gemstone dangling between her tits and ran for it. Problem was I wasn't a runner. And while the fuck-you boots were good for inspiring fetishes and concealing weapons, they didn't do a damn thing for speed.

I looked down, past her chest, to her empty hands folded at her waist. No purse. Had she left it at the bar? I thought back to her entrance. No purse. I'd been so distracted by her boobs and bling I hadn't noticed then.

What had the bartender said about ordering water? Short of pawning her necklace and earrings, Bettie wasn't buying anything tonight. Not a cosmopolitan and certainly not a hotel room. I swallowed my favorite swearword and smiled reassuringly.

"OK, you can come home with me."

So much for my professional code. Taking her to my place was a mistake, and I knew it. Unfortunately, my only options were using my ID to rent a hotel room, breaking into someone else's apartment, or calling it all off.

Tex was gone, and it was getting late. If I wanted to score tonight, it was Bettie or nothing.

We didn't say much in the cab or the elevator of my building. I berated myself for taking a risk. Sure, her jewelry would add some much-needed padding to my bank account. Convincing her she had lost her valuables on the way to my apartment rather than *in* my apartment could prove tricky.

Especially if she wasn't drunk.

Then again, I had plenty of booze at home.

"Can I get you a drink?" I asked, affixing the chain lock and clicking the two deadbolts into place behind us.

"We're locked in?" Bettie asked, her eyes wide with worry. I was beginning to think that was her signature look. "I don't like feeling...trapped."

"No, everyone else is locked *out*. Now how about that drink?"

Bettie slowly turned in a circle, taking in my sparse and admittedly unkempt apartment. "Water will be fine."

Shit.

"You sure I can't get you something stronger, my dear?" I asked, all but gritting my teeth.

Bettie collapsed onto the loveseat—an ironic name, given I was the only one who ever sat on it—and started weeping. I could work with that.

I went to her, draping an arm over her shoulder and

resting the other on her knee. "What is it?"

"You…" Sniff. "You…" Snort. "You're just so…" Sob. "Nice!"

If she only knew.

"And…and I don't even know your name!"

"It's Nic."

She brushed blond curls out of her face. "Is that short for Nicole?"

I shouldn't have been so surprised. Women tended to be better at sniffing out the double X chromosome. Or, more accurately, they're programmed to detect the Y. To pursue a mate or rebuff unwanted attention.

I faked a laugh. "No, not Nicole."

She waited for me to go on, and for some idiotic reason, I did.

"Veronica."

Bettie smiled a smile that would have made anyone else fall in love with her on the spot.

"You really are perfect," I said. Not because it was true, but because it's something women loved to hear.

Not Bettie, apparently. She shot up off the loveseat like something had bitten her on the butt. "No, Nic, I'm *not* perfect. I'm…broken."

There was a cue if I'd ever heard one. I rose and approached her slowly. Facing her, I put my hands on her arms—still hot despite not being flushed—so I could pull her into an embrace at just the right time.

"It's going to be OK, Bettie. Whatever is going on with you, we'll fix it…together."

She giggled and pulled me into a hug. Dizzy from the emotional rollercoaster that was Bettie and from how hard she was squeezing me, I nonetheless patted her on the back. I could either go the talking route or push my luck on the physical front.

Talking to people about their feelings wasn't exactly one of my strengths.

I drew back slightly, gave her the most sincere look I could muster, and went in for a kiss. She stiffened. I pressed my luck and my tongue against her lips. The gamble paid off. Her mouth opened. Her tongue started to move against mine.

While I enjoyed sexual release as much as the next human being, kissing never did it for me. The sounds, the sensations—the whole shebang felt far too alien to be stimulating. Worse, most women seemed to be slow kissers. It was all about passion, consideration, tenderness.

But not Bettie.

Her eagerness quickly outpaced mine. She kissed fast and hard. When more of her tongue ended up in my mouth than my own, I dropped my face to her neck and started mouthing the smooth flesh there. If things were shifting into hot and heavy, it was time to get to work.

Bettie threw her head back. Her laugh trailed off into an animalistic noise that made me cringe. Knees weak, Bettie backpedaled onto a chair covered with a pile of already-worn-but-clean-enough clothes.

Surrendering to the momentum, I fell with her and ended up straddling one of her legs. I buried my face into one breast. The cold, unyielding necklace pressed against my cheek.

Bettie continued to half laugh and half cry as I ran a hand along her thigh, up past the hemline of her silky white dress.

No bra above and no panties below. Maybe Bettie *was* an escort.

"Wait…" she moaned.

I didn't. If I couldn't slip the necklace and earrings off her while she lay in a drunken stupor, I'd do it during her post-coital nap.

"You can't…"

"Shhh," I said. "Shaved down there, huh?"

Bettie shot me a look that defied interpretation, as if fear and elation were warring for her very soul.

"Don't worry," I said. "I like a smooth—"

But she was *completely* smooth. All of her. It was like fondling an oversized Barbie doll.

I scrambled back. If I hadn't been so surprised, I might've drawn my gun. "What are you?"

Bettie self-consciously tugged at her dress. The idea of covering up private parts that didn't exist would've been amusing under other circumstances. Tears spilled down her cheeks, but otherwise she kept the hysterics at bay.

"I am Bettie." Before I could call her bullshit, she added, "Biomech Engine Testing Theoretical Imitation of Emotions."

"You're a goddamn *machine*?"

The voice was mine, but the words—the tone—was my mom's. She'd called me the very same thing when I was, what, ten years old? As if the stork had brought her a heartless replica instead of a real baby. As though my genetic programming was somehow my fault.

"I'm a prototype," Bettie said, suddenly cheerful.

I remembered the innovation conference Tex had mentioned. "Definitely not a sexbot…unless they forgot to finish you. Have to admit, they're getting awfully good at the AI though."

Bettie beamed. "I am an experiment in artificial *emotion*, not intelligence."

Something heavy slammed against the door.

"Bettie? You open this door right now!"

I recognized the voice. Not Bettie's boyfriend or her pimp. Her literal owner.

"Shit. Do you have some kind of tracking device inside you?" I asked.

Bettie, hands cupped in front of her mouth, stared fearfully at the door. Then the apartment shook as a shoulder or foot connected with the door again.

"Hold on," I called, running toward the sound and away from the emotionally unstable android in my living room.

As I fumbled with the locks, Bettie said, "You can't let him in, Nic. Please!"

I unbolted the door and opened it wide enough to see the man from the club on the other side, breathing hard. Calling him disheveled would've been a compliment.

"Hey, sorry about—*oof*."

I registered his wild sneer a moment too late. He shoved so hard the chain snapped off the door as he rushed me. By the time I brought my arms up to stop him, he was already pushing past. My hip hit the loveseat, knocking my feet out from under me and sending me to the hardwood floor.

"If you know what's best for you, you'll stay down," he growled before stomping over to Bettie.

I expected her to quail beneath his rage. Big eyes, sobbing, the whole mess. But she was just…numb. And she was looking at me.

"Voice commands aren't working," the man told her, "so I'm going to power you down manually."

Bettie didn't resist. Probably she couldn't. My mind raced as the man ran his hand up the back of her neck, positioning his fingers behind her ear. It could have been mistaken for a romantic gesture if not for the cold look in Bettie's suddenly lifeless eyes.

When he bent down to hoist Bettie over his shoulder, I shifted into a sitting position. Facing my bizarre houseguest and his expensive toy. And the expensive necklace that had just fallen onto the clothes-covered chair.

To keep him from looking back, I asked, "Do I get some kind of finder's fee?"

His grimace could've been caused by my comment or Bettie's weight. He adjusted his grip. "You're lucky I don't sue you for corporate espionage, not to mention aggravated assault."

In order for the assault to be aggravated, I would've had to use a weapon, intended to kill him, and/or inflicted a fairly serious wound. I chose not to correct him.

"So what now? You just take your crazy robot and leave?"

"Unless you want a shiner to match the one you gave me."

The hard look on his face suggested he would've welcomed the opportunity. I decided he wasn't the mad scientist who invented Bettie. Maybe some kind of security goon. One thing was clear though. I wouldn't be able to sucker punch him a second time.

"Just tell me something before you go," I said. "Why the hell would you give a robot emotions?"

His sneer returned, and in it I saw Tex's disgust, my mother's disdain, and a hint of the hatred I'd once harbored for myself.

"Someone like you couldn't possibly understand," he spat.

I didn't know I was going for my pistol until the thing was in my hand. His surprise was almost immediately replaced with fury.

"Someone like you," I repeated.

"If you know what's best for you, you'll put the gun down."

"Implying *you* know what's best for me?" I shook my head. "If *you* know what's best for *you*…meaning you don't want another hole in your dick…you'll put Bettie down. Now."

Muttering a stream of curses, my intruder-turned-hostage bent down and deposited Bettie beside the chair. Her head was all of four inches from a pair of stained underwear that wouldn't have looked flattering on anyone. I might've been embarrassed if not for the adrenaline coursing through my body.

Or if I had a tenth of the emotions Bettie did.

"You're making a huge mistake," the man in the suit said.

"No." I stood up and took a step closer to him. "Letting you walk out of here with something so valuable would be a huge mistake. About that finder's fee…"

He didn't roar. Didn't snarl. Without any warning whatsoever, he lunged forward. Startled, I pulled the trigger and watched him drop, straight back, at my feet.

"*That's* aggravated assault."

I waited a few seconds, keeping my gun trained on him. He didn't move. I approached and nudged him with the toe of my boot. No resistance. Lots of blood.

"Make that involuntary manslaughter. Shit."

I allowed myself a full minute to plot out various paths forward. Whether I called the police or waited for someone who heard the gunshot to do it, the ending wouldn't be a happy one. A plea of self-defense could work. But even if they didn't trace any of my prior thefts back to me, I'd be on their radar going forward.

The smart call was to grab the necklace and blow town. I glanced at the diamond, then at Bettie. Sure, she was valuable—even a malfunctioning robot had to be—but I couldn't carry her. Better to leave her lying on the floor.

She'd be reclaimed by whichever stupid company spawned her.

Doomed to be reprogrammed or destroyed because she wasn't exactly what they wanted.

Kneeling beside Bettie, I traced the back of her ear until I felt a slight bump. Several seconds later, Bettie sat up with a gasp. Like she had just woken up from a nightmare. Like a person.

"Nic?"

"We have to get out of here. That guy who came for you…well, I shot him."

Her eyes nearly doubled in size. "Is he *dead*?"

"Yes, but don't even think about turning on the waterworks." I held out a hand. She took it, and I pulled her to her feet.

I felt the android's eyes boring into me as I threw some clothes, all my money, and a bottle of bourbon in a knapsack. Over my shoulder, I asked, "Why give emotions to machine, Bettie? Why would somebody do that?"

"My maker believed intelligence operating in isolation is dangerous. Producing AI without other human attributes would eventually result in disaster."

I snorted. "Thought he could stave off a robotic uprising by building a neurotic android with tits, did he?"

She regarded me curiously as I slipped the necklace into my pocket. Tossing the dead man's wallet into my bag, I said, "Time for us to go."

Bettie followed me to the doorway. "Why are you helping me?"

"Because you're special. No, wipe that dopey smile off your face, Bettie. You're not my fucking soulmate. You're one-of-a-kind. *Valuable*."

"But I'm broken," she protested.

I kicked the door shut behind us. "Ain't we all, sister."

The Lake Road

Felix gazed upon the pelicans circling Lake Winnebago, marveling at their improbable grace. According to his predecessor, the birds had only recently expanded their migratory routes to include Wisconsin's waterways. Yet Felix thought the gangly birds would have looked out of place in any sky.

He could relate.

Turning away from the brownish-blue lake, Felix stretched his wings and leapt up from the rock-studded shore. He slowed his ascent after a few hundred feet. In the predawn half-light, Highway 45—or the Lake Road, as the locals called it—looked like a long, winding serpent. There were no travelers, not yet.

Another glance at the lake revealed the flock of pelicans bobbing contentedly on the placid surface. Alistair had suggested starting the day here rather than at the busier, multi-lane highway in the distance. Now he understood why. An orange glow reached up from the horizon, undulating through the gently rippling waters. Felix yearned for the caress of sunlight across his silvery feathers.

But even as the first rays of light washed over him, he was forced to tear his gaze away from the exquisite sunrise. The loud engine, while detrimental to the morning's serenity, should not have alarmed him. Beneath the pounding pistons and belching exhaust, however, he heard an unearthly voice.

Felix cleared the miles in the twinkling of an eye. A solitary vehicle hastily wended along the Lake Road. He maintained his altitude and searched for signs of the Enemy but spotted no spirits aloft. None lurked on the ground either.

Which could only mean the wood-paneled station wagon had an unwelcome passenger.

Felix swooped down and passed through the faded navy-blue roof as though it were an intangible illusion. Then he substantiated once more, poised on his haunches in the passenger seat.

It took all of his strength to ignore the vile sensations emanating from the back. Hand on the pommel of his sword, he studied the driver, a young woman with disheveled hair, bloodshot eyes, and frowning lips. She squeezed the steering wheel with two white-knuckled hands.

...can't be late...not again...why didn't the alarm go off?...stupid phone must've died again...no money to replace it...crap...did I leave it at home?...no it's in my pocket...but I should've charged it...shouldn't have stayed up so late...shouldn't have...

The car skidded around a sharp curve.

Felix took a deep breath—a fruitless gesture for his kind but one known to calm nearby humans. "There are worse things than falling behind. Slow down."

The woman eased up on the pedal.

From the backseat, a voice like screeching tires said, "No, you can still make it on time! Go faster!"

Felix spun around, unable to contain his bright fury. Stale yellow eyes squinted against his radiance. Rather than brace for battle, however, the imp merely folded his spindly arms across his mottled, leathery chest.

For some reason, the demon wore a seatbelt. Felix doubted he would ever understand fiend humor.

"Haven't seen you around before," Speed Demon said. "You Alistair's replacement?"

Felix wrinkled his nose. The imp stank of the worst kind of pollution. Turning back to the woman, Felix said, "You need to slow down. If you cannot afford a new phone, you certainly will not be able to pay a traffic citation."

Speed Demon snorted. "That ain't gonna work, pal. Cops almost never bother with the Lake Road, and the kid knows it."

Felix slid his hand from the sword's pommel down to its hilt, but he didn't draw the weapon.

Times had changed since his last assignment. Back when he was charged with protecting pilgrims bound for sacred destinations, spiritual warfare had been a daily occurrence. Felix had dispatched adversaries far mightier than Speed Demon—true terrors that made the imp in the backseat seem like a gnat by comparison.

But the Crusades were long past. Angels were rarely assigned to individual sojourners anymore. As the humans had multiplied over the centuries, the corps of holy guardians had adopted a more territorial approach to defense.

And while keeping a watchful eye on commuters in southeastern Wisconsin resembled his old role to a small degree, he couldn't help but think his talents were being squandered here.

Speed Demon glanced at Felix's sword and chuckled. "You're a hot-tempered one. And those wings! Very old school. Haven't been down here in a while, eh? Didn't

Alistair tell you that if you send me to the Pit, you'll get in just as much trouble as me? Maybe more!"

Unwilling to suffer the imp's sneering expression a moment longer, Felix turned around. He silently dared Speed Demon to attack him as he settled into the passenger seat, though Felix knew he wouldn't.

Because the imp was right.

Spiritual battles tended to make nearby humans more excitable, more unpredictable, and more dangerous. When Heaven had implemented a new strategy—one that relegated combat for crises only—the Enemy had done likewise. Felix knew better than to question his orders, yet he suspected the demons benefited more from the cease-fire.

"Every human knows right from wrong," Alistair had reminded him during his tour of the Lake Road. "An angel's job is not to eliminate the choice between good and evil, but to help steer them toward the better path."

The woman to Felix's left chewed her lip. Her frantic thoughts rivaled the velocity of the car.

"Faster, girl. Faster!" Speed Demon shouted, bouncing up and down in his seat.

"Do not be reckless," Felix told the woman. "If someone steps onto the road, you could not hope to stop in time."

As if to emphasize his point, a yellow sign bearing the silhouette of a stag whizzed by the passenger-side window. The woman ignored both the sign and his admonishment.

Felix took another deep breath to pacify the driver, though it sounded more like a sigh. How he longed to impale the tiny fiend with his broadsword! If this was to be a battle of words, a messenger angel would have been better suited to the task.

Why had he, one of Heaven's finest warriors, been sent to the middle of nowhere after being away from Earth for so long?

"Hey, Feathers, why do you care if this chick gets in an accident anyway?" Speed Demon asked. "The only reason she's in such a hurry is 'cause she has to get home before her boyfriend does. He works third shift, and she's been screwin' some dude in Fond du Lac the past few weeks. Wouldn't it serve her right if she took a one-way trip through the windshield?"

Felix focused on the driver, looking through her frazzled exterior and into her flawed interior. Jessica Matthews was a twenty-year-old nursing student at UW-Oshkosh. Her next class, scheduled to begin in less than half an hour, was taught by a professor with a reputation for wrecking GPAs.

No boyfriend. No indiscretions.

"Liar," Felix muttered.

In the rearview mirror, Speed Demon chortled obscenely, kicking the back of Felix's seat with his stubby legs. No, Felix would never understand fiend humor.

Suddenly, the station wagon whirred around a bend and was bathed in the flashing red lights of a much larger vehicle.

Jessica stomped on the brake.

Felix froze.

Speed Demon squealed in delight.

The station wagon came to a stop mere inches from the school bus's rear bumper.

"Jesus!" Jessica gasped.

Felix frowned at the woman. "Maybe now you will drive at a safer speed?"

...too close...I could've been killed...what if I had hit a kid?...God, that was stupid...I have to slow down...no

class is worth dying over…

Before Felix could decide whether Jessica or someone on the bus had been the intended target, he was distracted by a foul oath from the backseat. Speed Demon pulled himself into a standing position without bothering to remove the seat belt, which sank through his suddenly insubstantial form.

"Oh well," the demon said, flashing a despicable grin. "Maybe next time."

The imp jumped, frog-like, through the top of the station wagon and landed clumsily in a ditch. Felix watched Speed Demon bound away, leaving a trail of black, tarry stench in his wake.

The angel launched himself into the air, intending to stalk the wretched spirit from a distance. He glanced over his left wing to bid Jessica Matthews a silent farewell…

…and saw a fiend ten-times bigger than Speed Demon drop like a boulder onto the hood of the station wagon.

"Wrath!" Felix gasped.

Surrendering to instinct, he drew his broadsword. The blade shone with the brilliance of a million suns as he charged. The enormous demon reared his ram-horned head and roared a challenge of his own. His unsheathed scimitar bled darkness.

Felix had faced Wrath on countless Byzantine battle-fields throughout the twelve and thirteenth centuries. Back then, the fiend captain had compelled Christians and Muslims alike to commit murderous deeds, exterminating all reserves of patience and compassion in the hearts of men.

"Is that you, Felix?" The behemoth's voice boomed across the countryside. "We haven't sparred in nearly a millennium. I assumed Heaven had retired you after your failure."

Felix, who had seen too many comrades fall beneath that midnight scimitar, ignored the jibe and swung his broadsword. Wrath parried. Then, grinning and growling, the demon threw himself into a series of swings and feints. Felix blocked, dodged, and counterattacked, determined to keep out of reach of the wicked weapon.

No matter what Felix did, Wrath wouldn't budge from his rust-covered perch.

Airborne once more, Felix circled the station wagon, which stopped and started at irregular intervals as it followed close behind the bus.

After several more passes, Felix gained some altitude and dove, flying straight at the demon with his blinding broadsword out before him—a flaming arrow aimed at the fiend's heart.

Wrath held his ground. But he sidestepped at the last second and swung his scimitar in a powerful arc that would have cleaved Felix in half if he hadn't pulled out of his dive an instant earlier.

Felix's landing was inelegant, but he quickly drove the tip of his broadsword into the hood. Pivoting suddenly, he slammed a foot into the demon's chest. The impact sent Wrath falling through the windshield, past two rows of seats, and into the station wagon's vast trunk.

Felix climbed into the passenger seat, astounded that the formidable Wrath hadn't seen the blow coming.

The demon scowled at Felix from between headrests, but when he spoke, he aimed his words at the driver:

"Why won't that damned school bus pull over and let you pass? Does he think he owns the road?"

Felix gripped the broadsword in his left hand and reached out for Jessica's shoulder with his right. Irritation radiated from her small, tense frame. He attempted to infuse her with patience—but failed. He gaped at his cold, powerless hand in disbelief.

"Ignore that ridiculous little stop sign of his and go around him," Wrath ordered.

...don't have all day, you jerk...must be nice making people wait for you...is holding everybody up how you get off?...I just want to get to class, you piece of...

Felix leveled his broadsword at the demon. "Still your tongue, Wrath, or I shall remove it!"

To Felix's surprise, the demon returned his blade to its scabbard and laughed, a mockery of mirth that could incense even the calmest of souls.

"No one has called me by that moniker in ages. I now go by Road Rage." He winced as he spoke the final two words, as though the new name were a toothache. "Go ahead and vanquish me. Maybe if you send me back to the Pit, I'll get reassigned. No shortage of wars today, and I get stationed *here*?"

Felix frowned, remembering a recent conversation he had had with Alistair. His predecessor, who clearly loved the Lake Road and its travelers, couldn't understand Felix's disappointment at his new post. Or his dissatisfaction with so mundane a mission.

The fact that Felix empathized with a demon filled the angel with shame.

"Have you lost your edge?" Road Rage's burning, sulfurous breath billowed into the front seat. "Is that why you've been hiding in Heaven all these years? Enough. Let's put an end to this pathetic skirmish."

Felix stiffened as Road Rage crawled over the divider and into the backseat. Unlike the pitiful Speed Demon, his bulk filled the entire width of the vehicle.

"What are you waiting for?" Road Rage yelled at Jessica. "Everyone walks all over you. Grow a pair and *pass* this asshole already!"

...screw it...the next time he stops, I'm gonna go...

Road Rage flashed a dark, jagged smile, and suddenly Felix understood his peril. Since Speed Demon had failed to smash the station wagon into the back of a bus, Road Rage was instigating a head-on collision.

For reasons Felix could not guess, the Enemy wanted Jessica Matthews dead.

"No, do not pass the bus!" Felix shouted, but Jessica wouldn't—*couldn't*—listen. Like the demon, she was breathing loud and fast. Her face was twisted in fury, a sickening parody of Road Rage's fierce visage.

"You have lost, Felix," Road Rage proclaimed.

Felix looked from demon to driver. Road Rage's hold over her was too strong for him to break. But how could he destroy the demon's influence without dispatching his ancient foe?

What use was Felix to this world without his flaming sword and righteous indignation?

While patrolling the Holy Land, he had earned a reputation for stealing victory despite overwhelming odds. His adversaries claimed he was just lucky, but Felix knew it was his tendency to do the unexpected that gave him an advantage—albeit at great personal risk.

During his last encounter with Wrath, Felix had been protecting a handful of innocents from bloodthirsty brigands. He confronted the band, expecting to find only one or two demons among them. However, a small army of the fiends had ambushed him. He stood his ground, slaying the most eager of the host.

Felix's determination had nearly been his undoing.

Drenched in the fetid blood of fallen fiends, with one of his wings torn and his broadsword dulled, Felix retreated back to the pilgrims. Out of desperation, he created a sandstorm and led his charges into it, shielding them with his battered wings.

Even Wrath's intoxicating taunts couldn't convince the bandits to brave the storm. Felix had outsmarted them all.

But that wasn't enough.

When the winds finally settled and the pilgrims were safe, he sought victory, vindication, *vengeance*. Ignoring his injuries, he dispatched demon after demon with zeal. Wrath alone had escaped his fury.

Only now, so many centuries later, did Felix finally realize he had actually lost.

Leaning against the passenger window, Felix looked up, seeking forgiveness and divine inspiration. There were no storm clouds today, no clouds in the sky at all.

Just a flock of pelicans taking their leave of Lake Winnebago.

"Now!" Road Rage roared.

...don't give a damn about your flashing lights...I'm making my move...

Jessica yanked the steering wheel to the left and pounded the gas pedal into the floor. The vehicle crossed the center line.

Bowing his head, Felix said, "I am sorry."

Something struck the windshield with a thud. Cracks spider-webbed out from the point of impact. Jessica braked hard. A flurry of white feathers rained down on the station wagon.

"What the hell?" the woman and demon asked as one.

A tanker truck blasted past them, nearly sideswiping the station wagon as it veered away from them and onto the gravelly shoulder. The blast of its horn faded as the dust settled.

The station wagon sat motionless halfway between lanes.

Felix walked a few paces from the vehicle and knelt beside the mass of blood-soaked feathers, splintered bones, and a bulbous beak. He touched the dead pelican and said a prayer. Warm, golden light engulfed the bird. He smiled as it stood up, cocked its head at him curiously, and flew away.

A voice like war drums thundered above him. "This isn't over."

Standing atop the car's hood, Road Rage towered over him. Felix positioned his broadsword to parry the attack, but the demon's scimitar remained sheathed.

"Finish me," the fiend commanded.

"No."

"Do it, Felix, or every denizen of the Pit will learn of your cowardice!"

Felix slid his broadsword into its scabbard. "I will not be provoked. Not this time."

Eyes bulging, Road Rage started to shake. He raised his massive fists and howled. The demon swelled to nearly twice his original size before bursting into a mushroom cloud of noxious smoke.

When the red haze dissipated, the fiend was gone.

Felix approached the driver's side window. Inside the car, Jessica trembled. Her face's angry flush had wilted to a sheepish white.

He reached through the window and gave her shoulder a reassuring squeeze. "You are safe now."

The woman stiffened. Then he felt the tension drain away as a wave of warmth flowed from his outstretched hand into her body.

...oh thank God...thank you...thank you thank you thank you...

Felix waited for Jessica to ease the car back into the right lane before lifting off. Gliding on heavenly currents, he scanned the vicinity for more foes.

For the moment, all was calm. Gazing down at the Lake Road, he followed Jessica Matthews as she resumed her trek northward. He didn't know why she was important. He didn't need to.

"I will protect you, and you will end up where you are meant to be," he promised. "We both will."

Suspect 814553

The drone smashes the open door with its pneumatic mallet, scanning the room for hazards. Looking through its eyes, she confirms the text readout in the corner of her vision.

No artillery. No accomplices.

Never are in these cases.

She slams her holo-read shut and strides into the room just in time to see the suspect leap from his chair, nearly toppling the flimsy-wheeled contraption in the process.

The man looks from the drone to her to his stationary screen—an archaic monitor with more surface area than digital depth—as though deciding whether he should depower the device or leave the incriminating evidence on display.

In the end, he hangs his head and murmurs what might be an apology.

He manages only the first syllable before she signals the drone to deliver its payload.

The tranquilizer peters out after a couple of hours. By this time, the suspect is restrained in a state-of-the-art hydraulic chair designed for discomfort. A single halogen bulb fires blue-white light down onto him, obscuring the rest of the small room in impenetrable shadow.

"Oh no oh no oh no," the man mutters.

Denial will get you nowhere, she thinks but instead says, "Suspect 814553, you have been detained by the U.S. Department of Public Protection & Integrity."

The suspect starts to sob.

She rolls her eyes. A pointless gesture. Even without her anonymity helm, he never would've been able to see her from the safety of her remote interrogation pod.

She says, "Is there anything you wish to confess before questioning commences?"

He answers with a moan.

"Very well, Suspect 814553. We'll start with an easy one." She swipes through glowing green menus that hover before her. "Can you verify that you are the individual captured in this vid?"

She observes him as he watches the hologram that blooms in the darkness encircling him. His eyes widen, then clench shut, as the scene from two hours ago replays.

This time, reading his lips, she thinks that maybe he had been about to swear, not say he was sorry.

The timestamped version of the suspect collapses as the drone's tiny ordnance punctures his neck. Next, she sees her own hand reach past the drone's lens and clamp around the man's ankle. For the final few seconds of the video, the drone records her walking back through the broken door, pulling the suspect unceremoniously behind her.

"Suspect 814553?" she prompts.

"Yes…" He sucks in a ragged breath. "Yes, it's me. Are you the one who—?"

"I am the interrogator, Suspect 814553. As such, *I* will ask the questions."

A trail of snot slides down to the man's upper lip. She

sees his right hand jerk, but the plastic alloy of the manacle gives no quarter.

"Please," he whispers. "This has to be some kind of mistake. I'm—"

"Joseph Howard Milner, born November 3, 2025 in Madison, Wisconsin and current resident of 27 S. Willowbrook Drive in Port Washington, Wisconsin."

When he doesn't respond, she asks, "And the aforementioned address is where the recording was captured, correct?"

He swallows hard. "Yes. In my basement."

In her rookie days, she might have fired an accusation his way next. But she's learned over the long, trying years that those suspected of this particular crime have a stubborn streak. Worse, their proclivity for fabrication flares if the bald-face allegation is introduced too soon.

Better to circle around the charge, giving the suspect time to invent and dismiss an array of excuses—and stew in anticipation of the terrible, terminal blow.

"Suspect 814553, state for the record your occupation."

"Teacher…"

"Be more specific," she says.

"I'm a lecturer at the Nationalized Institution of Higher Education…in the School of Language & Communication, Virtual Campus."

She traces a shape around the display of the man's head and pulls the hologram toward her, providing a closeup of his sweat-slicked face. "And it's in the capacity of a lecturer that you teach Standard Legal Composition, Advanced Syntax for Compliant Communication Channels, and Universal Attribution Encoding…correct?"

"Correct."

"How long have you worked for the NIHE?"

He pauses before saying, "About six years."

"How long have you been a licensed educator in your discipline?"

"The same…six years."

She leans forward, not missing a beat. "And how long have you engaged in the prohibited practice of fabricating unsanctioned documents within the United States?"

"What? No! You…you have it all wrong. I never—"

With another sigh, she flicks her thumb and watches his teeth clench. She pans out and sees his whole body has become as stiff as the obtuse chair, which had just sent a pulse through the suspect.

Not a shock per se, but a muscle-stimulating frequency meant to debilitate and disorient the suspect.

Before he can regain his wits, she rewinds the vid, stops on a frame, and zooms in on the screen he had been using before the drone and she entered.

"Suspect 814553, can you please tell me what was displayed on your screen when you were detained?"

The man stretches out his jaw as though testing out his mouth before he answers. "I…I'm not sure…"

She doesn't need the chair's biometer readout to tell her he's lying. But she doesn't call him on it. Not yet. Let him savor the slim odds that he might somehow talk his way out of a conviction.

"Were you grading your students' assignments?" she prompts.

His brow furrows as he says, "No…"

"A correspondence from a colleague, perhaps?"

He doesn't answer immediately, and it's as though she can peer into his brain and see individual synapses fire while he calculates his chances of blaming the contraband on someone he knows.

At last, he says, "No…as a matter of fact, I wasn't sure

what I was looking at when you barged in. It could've been a computer virus for all—"

She flicks her thumb, cutting off the falsehood mid-sentence.

While she waits for his muscles to relax, she hopes that last pulse was enough to convince him to stop wasting her time and simply confess.

She knows he won't though. His kind never do.

The suspect's wide eyes shift from side to side, taking in only darkness. She waits. He's afraid to speak, not wanting to risk another pulse, but also using this time to devise a lie that might fool her. She'd bet her life on it.

Burying her impatience beneath professional resolve, she continues to wait. The translucent numbers in the corner of her vision tick away until five full minutes have passed. During that time, the man cries some more, makes a few noncommittal attempts to express how great a mistake has been made, and grows quiet once again.

She waits another three minutes before unmuting her mic. "You couldn't have contracted a computer virus because you were interfacing with a nonnetworked device. And that is a crime."

The suspect smiles—actually *smiles*—when he says, "I know...I know, and I'm sorry. I'll pay whatever fine you think is fair."

She waits.

"And you can keep it. The computer, I mean. I don't need it back. Destroy it or...whatever."

She waits some more. His heartrate ratchets up into a new, red-tinged, bracket.

"I don't even know what's all on it," he continues. "I got it from a friend...more like an acquaintance actually ...a long time ago. I found that file just before you got there. I don't even know what I was looking at!"

Even though she has no compunction with watching the liar sweat it out, she triggers the dermal infusion embedded in his manacles, sending an endorphin-rich cocktail into the oblivious man.

Whatever it takes to make him confess.

"Suspect 814553, are you stating for the record that you cannot identify the contraband found on the device taken from your home?"

"Yes! Because it's not mine!"

"Your statement has been logged," she says resignedly.

The suspect's grin widens. "Oh, thank goodness. Does that mean you're going to let me go?" he asks, his voice catching on the last word.

She allows herself a small smile. "On the contrary, Suspect 814553, you have logged a provable lie. Even though the device in question was not networked in a traditional manner, our surveillance bots have been remotely connected to it for the past three months, during which time you have spent on average of 43 minutes per day with the illegal file open and in use.

"Moreover, we can show through keystroke transcripts that you are, in fact, the author of the dissenting, *dangerous* story."

He starts to argue, but she has already muted her helm again. She knows the suspect will spend the next hour or more arguing his innocence and even attacking her and the Department of Public Protection & Integrity for their actions.

But she has had enough of Suspect 814553 for one day. Let him talk until his throat is dry. After a restless night in the chair, he will be more pliable.

Fiction can never withstand the test of time, whereas Truth is relentless, she thinks with a grin.

*   *   *

The next morning, she watches Suspect 814553 for a few minutes before making her presence known.

The chair permits microsleeps, but as soon as he reaches REM, the dream-quashing pulse courses through his body. His eyes open. His mouth curls into a trembling frown.

It's during one of these moments of discombobulation and despair that she unmutes her helm.

"Good morning, Suspect 814553."

"Joe," he says with a drawn-out sigh. "Please…just call me Joe."

She activates the sensors within her visor, projecting a green-lit outline of her helmeted head onto the darkness before him.

"Very well, Joe. Are you ready to tell me the Truth?"

He shivers and quietly tells her, "Yes."

Every aspect of the interrogation has been recorded, but she starts a second stream as protocol dictates—a backup in case the original file gets corrupted. Or deleted by chaos terrorists.

She sincerely hopes Suspect 814553 is on the verge of confessing his crimes in full. Sadly, there are other threats to public safety, and those other cases have been piling up lately.

Holding her breath, she watches the suspect lift his chin to look at her holographic helmet. Finally, he says, "I am the author of the document you found on my non-networked device."

"Be more specific."

He sighs. "I wrote the short story…in secret…in my basement."

"What is the title of the work in question?"

"'Secret Affections.'"

Despite a sudden surge of anger—the very name of the piece is a mockery!—she keeps her tone even, almost robotic. "What is the nature of the work?"

He sighs again. "It's romance…a…a love story."

"Is it an accurate account of actual events?"

He shakes his head.

"Vocalize your response, Suspect 814553."

"No," he replies curtly. "I made it up."

"Do you, therefore, plead guilty to the felony charges of producing fiction and possession of nonfactual information with the intent to distribute?"

She holds her breath. They have no evidence to support the second charge. The man has never made any attempts to contact other fabricators, either online or off. But every agent is urged to prosecute to the maximum extent of the law.

It was the most effective means of protecting the populace.

Anyway, why else would a criminal go to such lengths to create contraband if he didn't intend to share it with like-minded anarchists?

"Distribute?" the man asks groggily. "No, I wasn't going to *show* it to anyone. Not ever. For one thing it's really rough, and I wouldn't have wanted to get anyone else in trouble."

She nods, and her projected helmet echoes the movement. "Please state for the record the reason you committed the crime of manufacturing falsehoods."

Motive is little more than a formality—a form field to be populated as a matter of course—but there are times when the answer provides useful insight. Especially in cases where allegory, parody, or farce were incorporated to undermine the government or, worse, the Truth.

She leans forward as she awaits the answer to the question. Although she doubts she could ever truly understand the mind of a rebel, a perverse part of her wants to, if only to better understand the enemy hiding in plain sight.

Suspect 814553 chuckles humorlessly. "It's my mom's fault, I guess. Her mother used to read romance novels back when they were still legal—"

"Before the Misinformation Act of 2032," she supplies automatically.

"Right," he says, "before the government outlawed fiction in all of its forms. Mom passed away a few years ago, so I guess it's safe for me to say that she held onto a few of those books even after 2032, and I stumbled upon them at an impressionable age. You could say that's what got me interested in writing in the first place."

Heartbeat hammering, she wants to remind him that chronicling reality and making up events that never happened are two *very* different things.

Instead, she says, "And this interest in writing is what led you to take action against your government and deny your fellow citizens' the Right to Truth?"

He rolls his eyes, and it's all she can do to stop herself from thumbing up another stun pulse. Hard.

"Don't you think that description is a little...*extreme*?" he asks. "I mean, it's an innocent romance about—"

Before she can stop herself, she shouts, "A romance featuring two monoracial, cisgender, heterosexual, neurotypical characters. A romance that in no way acknowledges the complex reality in which we live. A romance with a clear agenda, subconscious or otherwise."

"No...no, you're overthinking it," the man argues. "That just happens to be the demographics of the main characters, but they could be anyone. This story *could* happen."

"But it *didn't*."

"This is insane! It's just a story! It can't hurt anybody!"

She glowers at the man, but the projected anonymity helmet betrays no emotion. A hundred arguments burst into her brain—everything from the threat of slippery slopes to tragedies from the lawless days before the Misinformation Act.

A time when news was more fiction than fact, and fiction fomented divisiveness and discord.

A time of anarchy that almost destroyed the nation.

A time before humanity realized that only Truth could transcend interpretation and manipulation.

But Suspect 814553 isn't worth the energy it would take to explain the horrible history that predates his birth. Anyway, no words from her will instill in him the proper measure of patriotism.

"Because you show no remorse for your crime, I am at liberty to impart the maximum sentence," she tells him.

He starts to argue again, but she has muted her inputs. Likewise, the oversized lines of her helmet have vanished from beneath the blaring halogen bulb.

She toggles over to the luminosity menu and kills the light entirely, plunging the small room into absolute darkness.

Angry though she is with Convict 814553, she doesn't relish in the suffering of others, not when the criminal broke the law out of ignorance, sheer naivete. The system failed him, but it isn't her job to educate this man—a so-called educator himself—and when she enters her passcode to administer his punishment, all she can feel is a pervasive sense of sadness.

As the chair reclines, preparing to perform a total creative lobotomy, she is already pulling up the details for her next case.

Drifters

As a kid, Allison liked to expel her breath in a steady stream of bubbles and sink down to the lake's sandy floor.

Enveloped by silence in that murky void, she imagined she was floating in outer space or experiencing a new state of being entirely, bereft of her body. Freed from the burdens of physics, the distraction of sensation.

Stepping out of her dreams gave her that same feeling.

Allison closed her eyes to shut out the subconscious-built scenery and concentrated on the cool emptiness of that childhood lake. The dream, which had seemed as substantial as anything in the real world, melted away. The air around her grew heavier or thicker. Wetter? But the cocoon of tranquil isolation embraced her for only a second before it was violently ripped away.

She held her breath, though she knew she wouldn't drown—*couldn't* drown—since she no longer had a mouth or lungs or a body at all. The idea of holding her breath was just a mental trick, an imaginary action that simulated what she would have done if any of it were real.

And how could she *not* compare the urgent pull of that invisible current to a raging river?

The first time she had wandered into this place—the space between dreams—she had fought the current, thrashing and gasping and struggling until she finally realized she wasn't in danger. That was when she learned she could steer her formless self through the flow of not-air-and-not-water by thought alone.

Those first few weeks, she eagerly plunged into the nearest pocket of reality to escape the minimalist state of being. Somehow she had understood, even in the throes of panic, that the blurry, bubble-like shapes pouring past her were other dreams.

She didn't start to suspect they were *other people's* dreams until she penetrated the flimsy skin separating them from the storming emptiness and spent some time wandering the unfamiliar landscapes populated by strangers.

After a month of exploring those random dreams—testing how much she could control without drawing too much attention to herself and accidentally waking up the dreamer—she tested a new hypothesis:

With enough concentration and persistence, could she find a dream that belonged to someone she knew?

Eventually, with lots of trial and error, she found Matthew's dream.

Tonight, she once again focused on his kind eyes, the shaggy brown hair that had grown past his collar since he moved away, and the endearing white scar on his upper lip—a permanent memento from when he had fallen out of her treehouse.

Grasping that image tightly in her mind, the current tugged her in a new direction. She relented. Seconds later, she found herself racing through the gray void toward a specific bubble and let the momentum sweep her into the dream.

Thanks to many nights of practice, she didn't fall from the sky. Instead, she approached slowly, allowing the dream to take shape around her. She kept to the edges, where details were sparse, where she could make sense of the setting stretched out before her.

Looks like a park. A big one. Central Park maybe?

Allison scanned the pathways and grassy areas, but she couldn't see Matthew anywhere. She took a few steps forward and shivered. Whenever she entered someone else's dream, she was always wearing the same white T-shirt and jeans. She closed her eyes and pictured a gray sweatshirt to shield her bare arms from the crisp autumn air.

When she opened them, the warm hoodie was there, zipped and hooded to hide her face.

She pushed her fists into her pockets and walked at a casual pace. It wouldn't take long to find him. While the fringes of every dream faded into nothingness, the center was the most vibrant, and that core always formed around whoever was having the dream in the first place.

All she had to do was keep moving toward where the scenery was most vivid.

I wonder if he'll be dreaming about Bliss tonight.

She hoped not.

The ghosts of skyscrapers towered in the distance, but as she followed a paved walkway, the trees throughout the park began to transform, their dull gray leaves bursting into the colors of fall. A jogger passed her, steam puffing out of his mouth with every quick, shallow breath. To her right, two children kicked a soccer ball back and forth.

Allison kept walking. She had given up trying to determine whether these miscellaneous people—these extras—were based on people in the real world. They could have been acquaintances of Matthew's or strangers he glimpsed just once. Anyway, they never paid any attention to her, so why should—

Wait a second.

On her left, a bearded man in a brown sloping hat sat

on a park bench, reading a newspaper. Only he wasn't reading it. The man smiled at her, and a spider web of wrinkles blossomed around his eyes. He nodded a greeting.

She gave him a tentative smile but kept walking.

I must be getting close to Matthew if this extra is real enough to interact with me.

Allison found her old friend lying on a blanket at the top of a small hill. Hands folded behind his head, Matthew stared up at the sky. A wave of relief washed over her when further examination of the area found no sign of the woman whose online name had been Bliss—an evil temptress who had lured Matthew to New York City and away from their wholesome hometown.

Matthew's eyes were open, which, she supposed, they would have to be. It wasn't as if a person could sleep through his own dream. She inched closer to the red-and-white checkered blanket, which would have been at home at any picnic.

Except there was no basket, no food at all. And Matthew, who had always been a slim guy, looked like he could have used a meal. The topography of his ribs pressed up against his black, punk-rock T-shirt.

As her shadow fell over him, he said, "You just have to find the right cloud."

"What?" She averted her face to keep the gray fabric of the hood between them.

When he didn't immediately answer, she stole another glance. Matthew continued to gaze straight up at the sky.

"If you find the perfect cloud, you can fly," he explained.

The voice was all Matthew's, but the words belonged to someone else. An imposter. New Matthew.

Reluctantly, Allison leaned over him. Thin ribbons of

red crisscrossed his glassy eyes.

"Oh, Matthew...not again," she moaned.

He reached up, presumably to grab a cloud. Allison turned away, unwilling to watch sweet Matthew Karls dream while under the influence of whatever drug had its hooks in him.

She wiped away a tear and then jerked in surprise when she saw the man from the park bench standing only a few feet away, newspaper tucked under one arm and watching her.

"I thought I might find you here again," he said.

Allison's reaction to the man's strange declaration mimicked what she would have done in the real world: she ran.

A hundred questions assailed her as she put as much distance as possible between herself and the man with the newspaper. The details of the dream bled away around her. She sprinted into a fog that mirrored the haze obscuring her own thoughts.

How did he find Who is he and what does he Are there other people who can There must be because he said What if he's just part of Matthew's No He is real I could tell just by just by Oh God what's that up ahead?

She skidded to a stop. To her left and right were the faintest outlines of trees, light posts, and what might have been a garbage can. Directly in front of her was a solid shape that could only belong to a human being—a stark contrast to the white-gray nothing surrounding him.

"Please, Miss, I didn't mean to frighten you." The voice wafting from the fog grew louder as the silhouette drew nearer. "I was hoping you and I could have a chat."

Allison walked backwards, matching the man's pace. "Who...who are you?"

"My name is Milton." As he advanced further into the

core of the dream—and she retreated back into it—more and more of his features manifested: a charcoal overcoat, the baggy brown hat, hands that he held out in front of him in a placating gesture. "Perhaps we can have a seat over there?"

With his left hand—which, she noted, no longer held a newspaper—he pointed past her at the empty park bench, perhaps the very one he had been sitting on when she first saw him.

"What do you want?" she asked, unable to hide her suspicion.

He chuckled, and deep wrinkles formed on either side of his mouth. He wasn't an old man, she thought, but he wasn't young either.

"Well, I'm not going to mug you if that's what you're worried about. As you likely know, this isn't really Central Park, and any valuables you carry on your person would vanish as soon as I woke."

She took a few more steps back but stopped when she saw the bench inexplicably beside her.

"Surely you have questions," Milton said. "I'd like to answer some of them, if I'm able."

There was kindness in those bright blue eyes of his, and there was something in the short-trimmed, salt-and-pepper beard and mustache—and the smile wedged between them—that reminded her of Grandpa Greene. She wanted to trust him.

Or maybe she was just desperate to know what the heck was happening to her.

Allison took a deep breath. "OK, we can talk…but no funny business!"

The warm smile returned. "I wouldn't dream of it."

They sat down together, sitting at opposite ends of the bench and leaving plenty of space between them. Milton crossed his legs and turned to face her. She folded her hands in her lap and looked straight ahead, where people came and went in a silent, almost spectral manner. A flock of puffy clouds roamed the too-blue sky.

"If you find the perfect cloud, you can fly," Milton said.

She stiffened, drawing a breath across her teeth to produce an inverse hiss, and then looked at the man.

"That's what he said, right?" Milton asked. "Your friend over there?"

Allison sighed and looked away. "He's high."

High and probably lying in some New York gutter, having the time of his life here in La La Land while his real life is ending one brain cell at a time. Oh, Matthew, how did you end up like this? What could I have done to—

"He's wrong."

The statement brought her attention back to the stranger.

"You don't need the perfect cloud," Milton continued. "This is a dream. Anything is possible, including flight. However, traveling at the speed of thought is faster. That's how I was able to get ahead of you when you ran."

Allison nodded. "It's easy to forget that."

"Yes, it's all too easy for us drifters to forget what we're capable of, especially in dreams that so closely mimic the waking world."

"Drifters?"

Milton removed his hat and scratched the patch of scalp peeking through the black and silver strands. "That's what we call ourselves. Dream drifters. Oh, there are more technical names for what we do…dream telepathy…oneironautics…but 'dream drifting' rolls of the tongue so much easier."

He replaced the floppy brown hat on his head and

asked, "What do *you* call it?"

"I don't know. I guess I just think of it as visiting a friend. I haven't told anyone about what I can do, so I didn't need a name for it. They'd just think I was crazy, right?"

"Or worse, they would believe you."

The statement took her aback, but she had other questions on her mind. "I first realized I could...*drift* a couple months ago. At first, I thought I was losing my mind, or maybe the painkillers were messing with me. I had just had my appendix removed..."

She brought one knee up, tucked it under her, and swiveled to face him fully. "How long have you been a dream drifter?"

A faraway look washed over Milton, and his smile grew. "I've had lucid dreams for as long as I can remember. That is to say, I could control what was happening in my dreams. But I didn't *leave* my dreams until I was around your age...twenty-four or twenty-five."

Allison couldn't help but grin. Most people who met her assumed she was significantly younger than her twenty-two years—sometimes guessing as low as sixteen!—and here Milton actually estimated too high. She was liking him more and more.

However, her satisfaction quickly turned to suspicion.

What if he isn't guessing at all? What if he knows who I am?

"How did you find me?" she demanded.

Allison gasped as she, Milton, and the rest of Central Park were suddenly plunged into darkness. What little light was left stained her formerly gray sweatshirt a deep shade of purple. The clouds above locked together in a solid, opaque canopy.

In the distance, someone cried out in terror.

"That hardly seems like the perfect cloud," Milton muttered.

"Matthew!" She jumped up, ready to run to him—her first love, her *lost* love—but Milton caught her arm. "Hey, what do you think you're doing?"

"He isn't in any danger, Miss."

His calm tone only amplified her panic. She pulled away, and he released her. Without looking back, she ran toward the hill. Matthew lay curled up in a ball, pulling the plaid tablecloth around himself like a safety blanket.

"No no no no no no no no no no no," he chanted, eyes clenched shut.

"Matthew, it's OK. I'm here. Nothing can—"

His eyes popped open, and Allison again saw the tell-tale capillaries intertwining like tiny red rivers. "It's Him, Allie. God! He's found me, and He's gonna…gonna…"

Matthew let out a wild shriek and started to scramble away but got tangled in the tablecloth. Allison spun around and nearly fell to the ground beside him when she saw a pair of gigantic violet-black arms parting the clouds and reaching down toward them.

"I'm sorry!" Matthew yelled. "I'll never shoot up again! Oh God, nooooo!"

The colossal hands descended in slow motion. Simultaneously, the sky began to flash wildly as streams of colorless lightning snaked throughout the dense clouds. Something touched her shoulder, and she yanked away with a yelp, half expecting to find some avenging angel behind her.

It was only Milton. "Take a breath. This is a dream, remember?"

"It's a *nightmare*. I have to help him!"

Matthew moaned piteously, trembling inside his checkered cocoon.

"I'm afraid it's too late for that," Milton said. "That strobe effect means his mind is fighting the unreality of the situation. Do you see how little remains of the park?"

Allison looked around, and sure enough, the fog was engulfing them. All that remained was a shrinking island of grass around Matthew. Meanwhile, the lightning had spread from the purple clouds to the nothingness surrounding them.

"The dream is ending," Milton said. "Take my hand, and we'll leave before we're forced out."

Allison had been ejected from dreams before. Remembering the terrifying undertow—like the earth was being pulled out from under her—she grasped Milton's hand, leaving Matthew and the darkness-bleeding fingers of the would-be deity behind.

One moment she was standing in Central Park at the stroke of Armageddon and the next, speeding through the eternally gray currents. Up ahead, she saw the faint outline of Milton. If she concentrated too hard, she almost lost him, but when she relaxed, she caught him out of the corner of her eyes, and subtle details filled in.

The experience was almost as disorienting as the waterslide-fast velocity that sent a thousand dreams whizzing past her every second.

Allison lurched at the sudden appearance of a floor—not to mention her own two feet standing on it. Instinctively, she reached out to steady herself and grabbed a hold of the wooden table that stretched from one end of the room to the other.

As she studied the place, which was illuminated by a pair of candlesticks, she realized she was wrong to think of the room as a room. The ring of dense shadow surrounding them implied the space was much bigger than she could imagine. A wave of nausea compelled her to take a seat on one of the twin benches that framed the table.

"Ah, my apologies," said Milton, standing beside her. "I make the trip so routinely I sometimes forget how discombobulating it can be to traverse the dreamscape at such speeds."

He gestured at the empty table. "You should take a drink."

Allison blinked, and a silver chalice materialized a few inches from her hand. It shouldn't have startled her, but it did. The impenetrable darkness, the medieval feel of the table and cup, Milton's knack for making the impossible possible—the entire situation was giving her a creepy *Phantom of the Opera* vibe.

"What…what is it?" she asked, resisting the urge to sniff the cup's contents.

Milton chuckled. "Water, though you could make it something stronger if you prefer."

"Thanks, but I'm not thirsty." She wondered what would happen if she ran into the shadows or leaped straight up in the air to launch herself back into the gray current. Would he chase after her?

Milton sighed and took a seat across from her. "You'll have to forgive me. I haven't figured out the right way to do this. I can't blame you for being suspicious…oh, don't deny it. You've been looking around like a caged animal ever since we arrived. But you're not trapped here. This is just another dream. You can leave at any time."

The temptation to flee came on strong, but her curiosity proved more powerful.

"You said you haven't figured out the right way to do this. To do what?"

"To introduce myself. To explain what we know about dream drifting. To invite others to join our cause." His smile returned. "I'm something of a recruiter, you see."

How many other people can do what we do? How can we do what we do? Why have I never been able to do it before a few months ago? What's the point? How did you find me?

She had so many questions, but before she could ask any of them, she needed clarification on a bigger question. "What is your 'cause'?"

"Asking the tough one first, eh? Usually, people want to know the whys and wherefores of dream drifting, and I get to build up to the big proposal. Your shrewdness does you credit, I suppose.

"Some things I will not be able to tell you until you join, and even then, much of what we do isn't disclosed to all members."

"Is this a secret society or something?" she asked.

He sniffed in amusement. "Not in the way you might expect. We're sanctioned by the U.S. government, which has a penchant for keeping classified information... well...classified."

Taking in the ordinary man in the slouchy hat, she couldn't quite suppress a laugh of her own. "You're a secret agent?"

"I'm a *scientist*," he said. "I just happen to work for an agency that specializes in international security."

"Recruiting people like me?"

"That's one of my roles, yes."

"Recruit us to do what?"

Milton reached for a second silver goblet and took a sip. "My job is to find more consultants for this little project of ours. The more dream drifters we have in our ranks, the more we can learn about the phenomenon and the better we can prepare for any event in which a rogue drifter might make trouble in the dreamscape."

He took another drink and added, "That's my official mission. However, my chief interest is developing a community wherein we special few learn from one another in the spirit of scientific discovery and mutual benefit...for the greater good of mankind."

"Our perennial idealist."

Allison jumped. Cups weren't the only things appearing out of nowhere. At the opposite end of the table, a man wrapped in a long coat stepped out of the shadows. The top of the garment was trimmed with fur, and as he approached the table, the candlelight revealed the color of his eyes and cloak to be the same. She couldn't help but tense beneath his gray-green gaze.

"Sorry to interrupt," the newcomer added. "I didn't expect you would have company."

"That's part of my job, remember?" Milton replied. "I find *real* dream drifters...just in case you fail in your work."

The man in the cloak stiffened, his eyebrows arching higher on his considerable stretch of forehead. But just as quickly, his expression returned to a neutral state.

"I...I'm sorry. I don't know why I said that," Milton mumbled.

The stranger dismissed Milton's apology with a wave of his hand. "No offense taken. Just remember that you choose your level of involvement here, Borr. I understand that moral flexibility has been a challenge for you in the past. You can't pull away from the group and then accuse everyone of turning their backs on you."

Milton's eyes narrowed, and color flooded his cheeks. "This is nothing like my situation with the Lucid Dreaming Society, Earl. I—"

"Odin." The other man's voice was low, but it cut Milton off as effectively as a shout.

Milton blinked and followed the man's stare across the table—at *her*.

"Yes…yes, of course. How rude of me. I ought to make introductions." Milton gestured toward the man with the broad forehead and steely eyes. "This is Odin. His role within our organization is difficult to explain without additional context, but suffice it to say he is in a position of authority. Is your escort still about? I'm sure Baldr would love to meet our guest."

"She's a bit young, don't you think?" Odin asked.

Allison felt her own cheeks flush. "I'm not as young as I look. I'm twenty-two!"

"Nevertheless…"

"Is there something you came here for…other than insulting prospects, that is?" Milton asked.

Odin paused, cast a sidelong glance her way, and said, "We begin the trials with our first candidates tomorrow night. I would like to invite you to attend." Pause. "Unless, of course, you expect your other work will keep you occupied."

Milton sighed. "No, I will be there."

"Good night then." Odin turned and, without as much as a look at Allison, walked back into the shadows.

After several seconds of silence, she asked, "Is he gone?"

"Huh?" Milton looked from her to the far end of the table and back to her. "Odin? Oh, yes, he's left the Great Hall. He won't interrupt us again, though I can't figure out why he came here when he could have just…" He smiled at her. "Never mind. It's nothing that concerns you or our conversation. Where were we?"

"You called him 'Earl' at first but then 'Odin' after

that," she prompted.

"Ah, you caught that, did you? We're supposed to use code names. Mine is Borr, but just about everyone calls me Milton. I'm not a big fan of secrets."

"Yet you're working for a secret government project."

Milton blinked in surprised, but he must have realized she was teasing him because he chuckled. "That's a long story, and I'm afraid it's getting late. I can't pretend to know when your alarm is set, but I'd better give you the highlights before either of us wakes up."

"All right."

She took a drink of the water in spite of herself. What was it about Milton that made her want to trust him? Because he was nice—or at least nicer than Odin? Because he reminded her of her grandpa, even though he probably wasn't much older than her dad?

Because he wasn't, as Odin put it, morally flexible?

Milton cleared his throat. "Very few people can do what we do. Some have elected to be a part of this project. As I said earlier, it's my job to find more, not only because it increases our numbers, but also because it exposes more naturals to the code of conduct we've developed. There are those who would do great harm upon unsuspecting dreamers out there. Intentionally or unintentionally."

"What do you mean?"

"At worst, a dream drifter can intrude and learn information about the host. In the arena of espionage, there could be dire consequences. But even in more casual situations, barging into another person's dreams uninvited is an invasion of privacy and, therefore, wrong."

The heat she felt on her face had nothing to do with the nearby candles. She wanted to point out that he had barged into Matthew's dream too. But she knew the only reason he had been there was because of her.

To stop her from doing it.

Tears stung the corner of her eyes. "He needs help."

"I know," Milton replied, "but you can't help him this way, not in the dreamscape. It's not fair to him."

She nodded and watched wax drip down one of the candlesticks. Milton wasn't telling her anything she didn't already know. She had kept guilt at bay by telling herself two wrongs made a right, but the truth was she hadn't been able to reach Matthew anyway.

"I don't know why God bestowed this gift on us, but he did," Milton continued. "It's our responsibility to protect those who can't protect themselves. That, first and foremost, is our mission at Project Valhalla."

"So if I joined, I wouldn't be allowed to go into Matthew's dreams anymore?"

"Yes, we would insist on that."

The candles blurred as she blinked back tears. "And if I don't agree to join Project Valhalla, I'll be a rogue drifter?"

"Not necessarily, though if we thought you were up to anything malicious, we would try to stop you." Milton reached across the table and rested a hand on hers. She didn't pull away. "As much as I think you would benefit from our group...and vice versa...I can't force you to join."

She tried to focus as Milton spoke of fringe benefits and how her work for Project Valhalla wouldn't have to impact her life in the waking world. But even though a part of her was excited at the prospect of meeting other people who could dream drift and to learn more about her "gift," she couldn't help but consider what she'd be giving up.

And who she'd be giving up on.

"I have to think about it," she said at last.

"I understand." Milton stood up, wincing as he stretched out his legs. "See what I mean about how easy it is to forget this isn't real? There's no reason why I should have circulation problems here, but the mind defaults to a reality-based line of reasoning if we let it.

"Anyway, since I have plans tomorrow night, how about the night after next?" he asked.

Allison stood too. "OK…but where? I'm not sure if I can find this place again."

Milton looked thoughtful for a moment. "You probably could, but Odin and the others wouldn't want me to tell you how. Not until after you agree to join. No, let's rendezvous the same place as last time.

"Matthew's dream? But I thought you said it was wrong to intrude?"

"It is," Milton replied. "Think of it as a chance to say goodbye."

"But only if I join Project Valhalla," she pointed out.

Milton smiled that grandfatherly smile of his. "What can I say? I *am* an optimist."

Two nights later, Allison walked through the front door of a house she had visited many times in the real world.

The front hall and living room were almost as familiar as the one at her family's farm. Matthew's winter coat hung from the banister—despite the many times his mother told him to put it in the closet—and the large cross that hung opposite the door was slightly crooked. As she straightened it, Allison caught her reflection in the cross's silver surface.

The face looking back belonged to someone else.

She sighed, grateful she had maintained control of her disguise from one dream to another but also regretful that she was entering Matthew's old house as a stranger.

How many times did we used to play spy, using the old baby monitor as a listening device in order to foil your parents' nefarious schemes?

She started as the doorknob rattled behind her. Her smile faded a little when the man with the slouchy hat crossed the threshold instead of Matthew Karls.

"Hello again," Milton said.

"Hi."

They stood in awkward silence for a moment. The faint sound of chatter and clinking silverware came from farther inside, and Allison imagined the small dining room with its old pink carpet and needlepoint décor.

"Perhaps we should talk upstairs," Milton said, "so we don't disturb them."

As much as she wanted to sneak a peek at the scene in the dining room—to catch a glimpse of Matthew during happier times—she led the way up the creaky brown steps. Milton made far less noise as he followed.

Without thinking about it, she opened Matthew's bed-room door and walked in. The room was exactly as she remembered. She wondered if it was her memory or Matthew's subconscious that rendered the football posters and model airplanes in such stark detail.

Although she had sat on the narrow bed so many times before, she chose to lean against the dresser, almost knocking over a picture of Matthew, her, and a bunch of other teens on a whitewater rafting trip.

"Soooo," she drawled, "How did your experiment go last night?"

The question appeared to take Milton by surprise because he hesitated between pulling out the chair at Matthew's desk and sitting down. "Well, I suppose it was a success, but whether that's something to be celebrated or lamented is up for debate."

"Good for Odin but bad for you?" she pressed.

Milton's brow creased as he looked closely at her. "You seem different tonight…and not just because you've changed your face, though I suppose that is a statement in of itself."

"Well, you gave me a lot to think about."

"And?"

"As I see it," Allison began, "if I work with you, I'll have the opportunity to learn more about my abilities. I'll get an inside scoop on what the government is doing with dream drifting. And I'll be helping people. If I say, 'no,' I'll be on my own, and you or someone else from Project Valhalla will probably shadow me to make sure I don't do anything you don't approve of."

She took a deep breath and glanced back at Matthew's smiling face in the photograph. "A yes means I can't see him anymore. A no means I can…unless you stop me."

Milton said nothing.

"I won't lie. I'm very curious about Project Valhalla. And…I think you're right…about Matthew, I mean. It's not right for me to come here and keep an eye on him. Even though I mean well. It's selfish."

"Does that mean you'll join?" Milton asked.

"On one condition."

Milton's eyebrows rose as he waited for her to go on.

"I get to keep my identity a secret. You all use code names anyway, right?"

"Yes…yes, that's true," he stammered. "But all of the other consultants have consented to give me their names. No one knows one another's real identities, however. That information is kept in my custody. But I'm afraid the CIA will insist on having your true identity on file."

"Then I guess it's a no," she said.

Milton frowned. "Can I ask why your anonymity is so important?"

She looked around the room at the replicas of Matthew's possessions, the snapshot of his life as it had once been. "Because it's an invasion of privacy. I'm hoping you can teach me how to keep other drifters out of my head, but small good that will do me if the CIA can find me in real life. I don't want to have to worry about agents tracking me down if I accidentally break some rule."

And I don't want that creepy Odin guy showing up on my doorstep just because he can.

Milton opened his mouth as if to reply, but he didn't speak for several seconds. "I understand your perspective, and I respect it. I'm just not sure…" He sighed. "If you're so distrustful of our organization, then why join at all?"

Allison mentally willed away the blush she felt coming. "It sounds like you believe God gave us these abilities for a reason. I'd like to figure that out with you…but I don't want to sell my soul to accomplish that."

Milton scratched his head, wrinkling his hat. "Well said. I'm…I'm just not sure…"

Then something hardened in his expression, and when his eyes met hers, she saw a strength there that belied his otherwise mild appearance. "Perhaps I can make an exception in your case."

"Really?" Allison couldn't hide her enthusiasm. It hadn't been a bluff—more like a longshot. She had fully expected Milton would refuse her terms.

"Granted, I don't know a lot about you, but from what little I've gathered, you have a good heart. Some might call me naïve, but I don't see the harm in letting you keep your private life…well…private." A ghost of a smile tugged at his mouth. "Besides, I would like to think I haven't sold my soul either and that we always have a choice in the decisions set before us."

"Wow, that's awesome…thank you, Milton!"

"Don't you mean 'Borr'?" he chided, but there was no weight behind his words. "You and I are opposites in this regard. I prefer people use my real name, though it drives Odin crazy. We'll have to come up with your code name quickly, and I'm afraid our options are limited to members of the Norse pantheon."

"Norse? I don't know anything about Viking gods," Allison confessed.

"The good news is only a couple of the goddesses' names have already been picked. The bad news is the goddesses tend not to be as popular as the gods, so you probably have never heard of most of them." Milton sighed. "Frankly, many of them aren't very pleasing to the ear. So…let me think…there's Sif."

Eh.

"Freyja."

No thanks.

"Nanna."

Yuck.

"Hnoss."

Double yuck.

"Syn."

Hmm…

"Syn?" Milton repeated, apparently seeing a change in her expression.

Matthew—in fact, all of her childhood friends and most of her family—had called her "Allie" for as long as she could remember, never "Allison." It seemed only fitting that if she were turning a page in her life—and in some sense turning her back on Matthew and her old, ordinary existence—that she switch from the first syllable of her given name to the last.

Syn nodded.

"And am I going to have to get used to this new face of yours?" he asked.

She nodded again.

"A pity. I rather liked the freckles."

"So…what happens now?" she asked.

"We should proceed to the Great Hall and begin orientation," Milton said, "but I did promise you the chance to say goodbye to your friend downstairs."

Syn almost took him up on the offer. The thought of never seeing Matthew again, not in real life and no longer in the dreamscape, felt like a punch to the gut. She bit her lip to dull the stinging behind her eyes.

Sparing a final glance at the rafting photo—at Matthew's happy-go-lucky grin—she said, "I'll pass. He wouldn't recognize the new me anyway."

The Monster & The Mirage

Dinah knew it was a mirage.

She stopped, brought a waterskin up to her mouth and squeezed, silently imploring the gods for just one more drop.

Her prayer went unanswered. She might have cried, but she had no tears left. The only moisture to be found, it seemed, was the sweat that glued the heavy fabric of her *dhal'aho* against her feverish skin.

The nomads whose caravans skirted theses sun-scorched wastes had warned her of such phantom pools. She had dismissed their stories. After all, the traders also spoke of wish-granting spirits and roving corpses as matter-of-factly as camels and cobras. But weeks of wandering the desert had given her no shortage of oppor-tunities to reconsider, and she vowed that she would not be tricked again.

Running her parched tongue across cracked lips, she could almost believe the nomads' claim that mirages were created by the *shaeli v'ai*—the witches of the wastes—who reveled in tormenting trespassers.

But what if it wasn't a mirage?

She started forward, shaky steps taking her closer to the illusion. She hated herself for entertaining the idea that relief was possible—that life was a possibility—anymore.

Why not give up? she asked herself. Why not suc-cumb, as so many others had, to the barren land that, though no man ruled it, bore no shortage of wretched names?

Denying the heaviness in her aching limbs and the dizziness that made the sandy horizon sway like ocean waves, Dinah thought none of the desert's names came close to describing the depths of its cruelty. Even Harpies' Eyrie—a name that had caused her some restless nights as a girl—seemed like a sad joke as she willed her blistered feet to take step after step toward the mirage.

She knew the half-woman, half-vulture abominations from her nightmares weren't going to swoop down from the cloudless sky and rip her apart with their spear-like beaks and talons, though she understood how those who came before her, explorers who miraculously had made it back out of the desert to tell their terrifying tales at taverns from one end of the Empire to the other, might have mistaken their heat-induced hallucinations for reality.

Of course, those explorers hadn't ventured nearly as deep into Harpies' Eyrie as Dinah had.

She had risked everything on her faith that some rumors might prove more than rumors, had gone too far to turn back. And so she would die, not a quick demise at the hands of monsters, but the slow, sanity-stealing death brought by thirst. She would suffer the same fate as her dear Elias.

Because surely the mirage was, in fact, a mirage.

She didn't realize she was stumbling until she hit the ground. Pain pulsed from her knee up her leg, and she had bitten her lip hard enough to draw blood. She sucked in the warm, metallic liquid, savoring the wetness on her tongue.

It took all of her strength to rise again. She didn't

bother to investigate what had tripped her but kept her gaze fixed on the sparkling pool ahead. With death stalking her like the long, emaciated shadow at her back, she wanted only to confront the mirage, to prove to herself and to any witches who were watching that she had known it was a ruse all along.

Then she was falling again. The sand tore into her palms like tiny, searing daggers. She let out a scream of frustration, anger, and defeat.

It was over.

Lying there, she felt the earth's heat pierce her *dhal'aho*, cook her skin, and burn her bones. When she closed her eyes, she could still see the beautiful lie shimmering just out of reach.

Zef stopped suddenly. Surely her eyes were playing tricks! She glanced at her companion, who stood perfectly still with her spear in both hands, the sun-faded and much-scarred haft held diagonally across her body.

Mimicking the other woman's defensive stance—and hoping Led hadn't noticed her belated reaction—Zef returned her attention to the scene ahead, where motes of light danced upon the surface of a small pond.

However, her gaze didn't linger on the oasis, but settled on the prone form that lay several yards from their rejuvenating destination.

"What is it?" she asked Led, who had patrolled the borders for the past eight years.

"An intruder," Led replied in a low, even voice.

From a very young age, children were told of the creatures that lived beyond their borders—nighttime tales meant to keep the little ones in bed. While training to become a protector, Zef had learned the truth about those who sought to bring ruin upon their hidden homeland.

She clenched her spear's smooth, unblemished surface tighter and decided she much preferred the mindless creatures of her young imagination.

"You...you are sure it's not a lion?" she whispered.

Zef regretted the question as soon as it left her lips. Led's glare settled on her, and her cheeks flushed with shame. Of all of the other protectors, Led had been the most vocal in her concern that Zef was not yet ready to join a patrol. When Zef had volunteered to fetch water for the circuitous trip home, the patrol leader had assigned Led to be her partner, as if to spite them both.

Why do I keep giving Led more proof that I am weak? Zef wondered.

Led said nothing as her dark, piercing eyes scanned one end of the horizon to the other. She then removed the large pack from her back and started forward again, spear at the ready. Over her shoulder she said, "Wait here if you wish, but this one might not be as patient as your firstkill."

Zef recoiled as if physically struck. After another moment speculating why Led hated her so much, she dropped her own pack and followed. She didn't bother to retort. Few were faster with a spear than Led, and no one could outmaneuver her in a war of words.

Anyway, what could she say? All of her sisters knew she had hesitated on her first hunting trip, when she had wounded a small wildcat with her sling and had had to finish the kill with a knife. As the maddened, dying animal lashed out at her, she had nearly lost her nerve.

Led had every reason to question how she would react when faced with dispatching an outsider. Zef was wondering the same.

The two protectors advanced slowly. Zef prayed that Led couldn't hear her heart thundering in her chest. She took some solace in Led's confidence that the outsider was alone, though she half expected a host of brutes to leap up from the sands around them. There was no sign of movement whatsoever as they neared their quarry.

All-Mother be merciful, thought Zef, maybe the outsider was dead already!

Curiosity conquering her fear, she inspected the prone figure. The stranger was covered from scalp to sole in a parchment-colored robe stained with patches of dirt and sweat. The garb was far heavier than anything a protector would wear. Surely the outsider lacked knowledge of the ointment that guarded against the sun's sting. She could think of no other reason for encumbering oneself with such a covering.

Looking down at the vulnerable creature, Zef was simultaneously eager and terrified to see what the thing looked like under the tarp-like robe. She winced when Led nudged the outsider with the butt of her spear.

No response.

Led struck harder, causing the body to rock a little before settling back into its original position.

"Pity," Led muttered. "The sun did the job for us. But we'd better be sure…" She shifted her grip on the spear so that the weapon was poised, point-down, above the outsider.

"Wait!" Zef cried before she could stop herself.

Led whirled around, holding the long wooden haft against her breasts. Eyes wide, the woman searched for imminent danger. Finding none, Led's look of anxiousness turned into one of severe annoyance.

"Why did you stop me?" Led demanded.

"What if…what if…?"

But Zef couldn't articulate the urgent thought that had sprung into her mind with the power of a pouncing lion.

Surrendering completely to instinct, she knelt down and rolled the outsider over. Led started to protest, but then the two women gasped together as they beheld a face both beautiful and strange.

Her skin was so light—almost as white as clouds, Zef thought—and the bones of her face were very pronounced, particularly the nose, which protruded farther than any Zef had seen before. She forgot the delicate features, however, when she noticed the hair that disappeared beneath the hood. The long strands sparkled like the red-gold skies of a desert sunset.

Surely this was one of the All-Mother's angels!

At last, she tore her gaze away from the stranger and looked up at Led to gauge her response. The seasoned protector frowned, deep furrows forming between her thick eyebrows.

"Who could she be?" Zef asked.

Led mumbled something unintelligible.

"What—?"

"A trick," Led repeated louder, her eyes never leaving the outsider. "She is not one of us, and yet…"

And yet, thought Zef, the stranger bore no resemblance to the grotesque drawings of the enemy shown to all protectors-in-training. No, this was not one of the ruthless brutes that called the Cursed Lands home, not the enemy she had sworn to kill to keep the last refuge of civilization safe.

"But how—?" she started to ask, but Led raised a hand, cutting her off.

"Doesn't matter," Led said.

"*Of course*, it matters!" Though Zef took some satisfaction in that Led was also taken aback by the mysterious woman, she couldn't understand her apparent lack of astonishment at the implications.

"What if she escaped from the brutes?" Zef asked, rising to her feet. "She could be the descendant of one of our own, taken by the enemy long ago! Or perhaps there are other cities—"

"Enough!"

Zef took a couple of steps back and surprised herself by adopting a defensive stance. Led stood at ease, holding her spear in one hand, its head pointing at the heavens.

Of course she wouldn't attack, thought Zef. The consequences for attacking someone other than the enemy was severe, and engaging in combat with a fellow Sister of the Spear was punishable by death.

Yet the venom in Led's expression kept Zef rooted in place, weapon at the ready.

Led opened her mouth as if to speak but was interrupted by a sound at their feet. The outsider let out a groan that faded into a long sigh.

Then the stranger's eyes flickered open, and for one precious second, Zef saw a color that rivaled the lush greens of the Temple's gardens. The woman made another noise—it might have been a word, but between her weak voice and the pounding in Zef's ears, Zef couldn't be sure—and went still once more.

"We can't let her die," Zef said suddenly. She was looking at Led, but all she could see was the angel's pleading green eyes.

Led was silent for a span that seemed to stretch for eternity. When she knelt down beside the outsider and reached for her belt, Zef took a step forward. But Zef knew the jagged spearhead wouldn't reach Led's neck before Led buried her knife in the stranger's milk-white flesh.

In the end, all Zef managed was an inarticulate yelp.

But Led did not unsheathe her short blade. Instead, she

removed a water skin from her belt, lifted the outsider's head, and coaxed a few drops of liquid into the woman's mouth. Looking up at Zef, she said, "Help me carry her to the oasis."

"Oh, thank you!"

Led glanced at Zef's spear, still leveled at her as if ready to strike, and smirked. "We'll bring her to the Holy Daughters. *They* will decide whether she lives or dies."

Dinah awoke in a dead panic. She scrambled to her feet, reaching for the hidden dagger in the *dhal'aho* sleeve.

The sheath was empty.

Suddenly, the world began to spin around her, sending her to her knees. Her stomach rebelled, but she forced the hot, bitter fluid back down.

Her surprise that there was any water left in her body to throw up was dwarfed only by her amazement that she was alive at all.

She turned at the sound of footsteps behind her and drew back at the sight of a spear. But the face of the woman carrying the spear conjured up hazy memories of being carried, the taste of blissfully cool water, and a sound she had thought she would never hear again— splashing.

Behind the woman with the spear, the gibbous moon's reflection rippled on the surface of the pool. Dinah smiled. The mirage wasn't a mirage after all.

The woman with the spear spoke slowly and sooth- ingly in a language Dinah didn't recognize. Her skin was bronzed by the desert sun, resembling the complexion of the nomads whose caravans traversed the fringe of the Enlightened Empire.

Dinah had never heard of a place where women

walked about bare-breasted, but maybe the female traders she had encountered on her journey simply covered themselves before setting up in the bazaar.

"I'm sorry, but I can't understand you," Dinah said. "And even though you probably can't understand me either, I nevertheless must thank you for saving my life."

A second woman who sat on a rock beside the pool said something, and there was no mistaking the scorn in her strange words. As the two women talked—or argued, by the sound of it—Dinah studied her saviors.

The sneering woman on the rock was completely bald, while the woman at her side kept her dark brown hair cropped short in the fashion of the young boys back home. Both women were naked except for a loose skirt made of animal skin that wrapped around the hips and ended just above the knee. From a belt made of thick rope hung a knife, several water skins, and a few small pouches.

Each woman bore a large black tattoo of an upward-pointing spear, its shaft bisecting a hollow circle, on her left breast. Unlike the nomads Dinah had bartered with for her *dhal'aho* and other long-since-spent supplies, neither woman wore jewelry of any kind.

And if Dinah had harbored any doubts, the long spears confirmed these women were warriors.

She jerked back at the nearer woman's voice. How had she gotten so close without my realizing it? Dinah wondered.

As she spoke, the short-haired warrior pointed at herself, her companion, Dinah, and then at something unseen in the distance.

"Are you asking me to go with you deeper into the desert?"

The two women watched her silently.

"You want me…" She pressed a finger to her chest.

"…Dinah, to go with you…" She indicated the two other women. "…out there?"

Her saviors exchanged a look. The one closer to her smiled, but the bald one scowled and muttered impatiently.

The short-haired woman pointed at her and said a few words followed by "Dinah?"

"Yes, that's my name. Dinah."

The younger woman's smile grew. She placed the palm of her free hand on her own chest and said, "Zef."

Dinah repeated the unfamiliar name and added, "A pleasure to meet you, Zef."

Zef beamed and stretched out a hand toward the woman on the rock. "Led."

"Hello, Led," Dinah said, nearly laughing aloud at the absurdity of the situation. Really, she thought, *what are the chances these two travelers would happen upon me before I crossed death's threshold? And now they are going to take me deeper into the wastes, perhaps guiding me to the very place Elias and I—*

"Elias!"

Dinah jumped up, fought against the vertigo that assailed her, and frantically scanned the heavens for familiar constellations. When she was certain she knew east from west, she looked back the way she had come. The steady wind of Harpies' Eyrie had already erased their footprints, but she was certain she could find her way using the stars.

"Please," she said, looking once again at her unexpected companions. "We have to find Elias. He could still be alive. If we bring him water…"

All at once, Dinah noticed the two spears pointing at her. The bald woman—Led—had crossed the distance from the pool to Dinah swiftly and soundlessly. Zef eyed

Dinah uncertainly, but after a few seconds, her spearhead dipped downward. My sudden movement must have alarmed them, she thought.

For the first time, Dinah considered the possibility her new friends might not be friends at all and that trying to determine whether she was their guest or prisoner might well get her killed.

"The bastards damn her wishes," Led spat, shifting her glare from Dinah to Zef. "She has no say in the matter. She's coming with us back to the City!"

Zef resisted the urge to shout back. In as calm a voice as she could muster, she told her fellow protector, "She intends us no harm. I am certain of it."

"It doesn't matter what she *intends*," Led replied quickly. "Our responsibility is to bring water back to our Sisters. We lost the remaining hours of daylight tending to the outsider. I won't waste any more time on a fool's journey into the Cursed Lands!"

Zef took a deep breath and let it out slowly. She wanted to argue that she and Led would have needed a rest anyway before setting off to rejoin their patrol. But she couldn't deny the sense in Led's final point.

The oasis served as a marker, the farthest point from the City that any patrol dared go. As far as Zef knew, no Sister had ever ventured beyond it. If not for the promise of replenishing their water, Zef doubted anyone would have reason to wander this far into the desert, which was fraught with countless dangers—everything from two-tailed scorpions to the abominable brutes.

Yet Zef knew they ought to follow Dinah with the same certainty that had prompted her to save the outsider from Led's spear in the first place.

"What if she has a friend out there?" Zef pressed. "Or a child? You see how she keeps herself covered. If she is a mother, then it is our duty to—"

"What if she has allies waiting in ambush?" Led retorted. "*Our duty* is to our thirsty Sisters and to our home. *Our duty* is to take this outsider to the Holy Daughters and let *them* decipher her purpose here."

Zef turned to Dinah, who had been paying close attention to their debate. Her bold green eyes were wide; her face, grim. Somehow Zef knew that if they tried to take Dinah to their camp and, beyond that, back to the Temple, she would fight them the whole way.

And Led would be only too happy to subdue her.

Giving Dinah a faint smile, Zef said to Led, "You take the water back to our sisters. I will accompany Dinah into the desert, and when we return, we will catch up with you and the rest of the patrol."

"Has sand fever claimed your mind?" Led demanded. "The Sisters' Council would never forgive me if I let you walk into the Cursed Lands with this stranger…not to mention your parents!"

Zef clenched her fingers around the shaft of her spear and balled her other hand into a fist. Usually when Led or the other sisters mentioned her family, it was to ridicule her for her former life of privilege or for supposedly receiving special treatment. Why else would someone as weak and inept as Zef be allowed into the Sisterhood of the Spear? they would taunt.

But the almost reverent way Led had just spoken of her parents was worse than the ribbing the other Sisters gave her—much worse.

"If you *let* me go? And who are you to stop me, Led?"

Her companion blinked in surprise. Zef pressed forward.

"While you are a more experienced protector, you are not my superior," Zef spat. "Let the Council decide if I am to be praised or punished when Dinah and I return. But as the All-Mother is my witness, I will not allow your fear to get in the way of doing what is right!"

Led's jaw dropped. She appeared as stunned by Zef's boldness as Zef herself was. *How long have I been waiting to stand up to her and those like her?* Zef wondered. *How long has it been since I heard my voice so sure and strong?*

Arms crossed, eyes narrowed, Led replied, "Have it your way, young Sister. But if the brutes leave your bones to bake in the desert sun, I'll not join the hunt to retrieve them, not even if the blessed Matriarch and the High Magus alike command it!"

Led stomped over to the two supply packs containing the newly filled water skins. She tossed two of the bloated skins and their remaining ration of dried meat at the ground near Zef.

"Best not wander too far from the oasis," Led muttered by way of a farewell. She then hefted up the two packs, the muscles in her arms and back bulging from the weight, and began her trek back to the patrol camp.

Zef bent down and picked up the supplies Led had left them, adding the two water skins to her belt, which already hung heavy at her hips from her own refilled water skins. She removed a piece of jerky from the small pack and handed it to Dinah, who took it but did not immediately eat it.

Dinah said something in her funny-sounding language and gestured at the endless expanse of desert.

"Yes, we will go west," Zef said, placing a piece of jerky between her teeth before wedging the leather pouch in place between her belt and rump.

Dinah smiled, and Zef felt a warmth rush over her despite the chilly night air. She watched as the outsider attempted to take a bite of the dried meat, but it took several attempts before Dinah finally broke off a piece with her side-teeth.

Zef shook her head and smiled back. Where had this woman who had never eaten cured venison come from? What did people who lived in the desert even eat—if that was where Dinah was actually from?

Most of all she wondered how someone who looked so fragile could survive for any length in the Cursed Lands.

As Zef chewed her simple supper, Led's final words echoed in her head: "Best not to wander too far from the oasis."

Zef couldn't contest the wisdom in the seasoned Sister's advice. She and Dinah had enough food and water for two days, at most. If they didn't find whatever Dinah was looking for by sundown tomorrow, they would have no choice but to return to the oasis and, after that, to the Great Forest and, finally, the City, where they both would face judgment.

She prayed to the All-Mother that the journey into the desert would prove to be worth the risk.

Dinah had to believe the gods were smiling down on her. She could think of no other explanation for why Zef had not only saved her life, but also agreed to accompany her on her search for Elias.

The two women had walked in silence through the night. Every half hour or so, Zef would ask her a question —asking her if she needed to take a rest, she assumed— but Dinah waved her away.

She had drunk her fill from the mirage that wasn't a

mirage, and the leathery strip of meat had settled her stomach and renewed the strength in her limbs.

But after several hours of walking, the blisters on her feet burned again, and a cramp in her side complained more persuasively with every step. She defied the discomfort. There was a chance—albeit a very small chance—that Elias was still alive out there.

The gods had given her an opportunity to save him, and nothing short of a sandstorm was going to stop her now.

They walked by the light of the plump moon, whose light stole all color from the land. If she squinted, Dinah could almost fool herself into believing she was walking through a snow-covered meadow in her native land. From time to time, she even shivered, though she had spent enough time in the desert to know that every night brought a false winter.

She wrapped her *dhal'aho* tighter around her and glanced at Zef, whose bare skin bore no goosebumps at all.

Although their conversations were stilted at best, Dinah welcomed the company of the mysterious woman walking beside her—not only because of the care she had provided, but also for the riddle she presented. Trying to figure out who Zef was and where she came from was an invaluable distraction from the one question never far from her thoughts: would they find Elias alive or dead?

Legend spoke of a lost civilization in the center of the wastes. She and Elias had gambled their very lives on the faith that the ancient stories were true. No one could guess how far into the desert the hidden city stood, but finding Zef and Led seemed to suggest that people—not monsters —did, in fact, inhabit Harpies' Eyrie.

During one of their short breaks, the first rays of

morning crested the sandhills at their backs. The temperature rose with each passing moment. Beads of sweat tickled the small of her back. She wiped the filthy sleeve of her *dhal'aho* across her forehead and wondered if she would be pressing her luck if she asked the gods for a cloud or two.

Beside her, Zef reached for something at her belt, not a water skin, as Dinah had expected, but a leather pouch she had not noticed before. Zef dipped three fingers into the pouch and scooped out some shiny white cream.

Dinah couldn't help but stare as the woman began rubbing it first on her legs, then her arms, then her breasts and belly. The ointment made her skin glisten like the caramel sweets Dinah's mother used to make.

Zef said something, and Dinah quickly looked away, an apology on her lips. But when Zef repeated herself, her tone implying a question, Dinah turned to find the other woman facing away from her, a splotch of the milky cream standing out against her bronze shoulder blade.

"You...you want me to spread it across your back?" Dinah ventured.

Zef didn't reply, only waited.

"Oh...um...all right." Dinah tentatively brought her fingertips to the cream, and when they made contact, she nearly pulled them away. The ointment was cold—unnaturally so. How can something feel as cold as ice in this heat? she wondered. In the end, she was forced to attribute the uncanny quality to an exotic herb, much like how a sprig of mint cooled the tongue on a hot summer day.

Soon Dinah was using both hands to swirl the cream in broad circles across the canvass of Zef's back, reveling in the coldness that permeated her palms and spread up her own forearms. When she was done, Zef turned around and proffered the leather pouch to Dinah.

"So this is how you're able to walk around half-naked without the sun cooking you alive," Dinah said.

A sudden breeze stirred up the sands at her feet—a frosty caress upon her ointment-coated hands—and realized that Zef was feeling the same thing except across her entire body.

Dinah looked down at the filthy *dhal'aho*, which had absorbed her sweat and stink like a sponge. How she longed to be rid of the ill-fitting garment that chafed her and threatened to trip her when she least expected it!

"I don't know…" she began, but Zef, wearing a wide, bright smile, pushed the pouch into her hands. "I suppose I would be a fool not to trust you now."

Yet she hesitated. Although the nomads who sold her the utilitarian cloak had told her wear it over her blouse and riding pants, she had discarded the only outfit she brought from her homeland on her second day in the desert, taking some comfort in the air wafting up from under the hem and across her bare legs. Before long, she had begun to fantasize about removing the *dhal'aho* too, sunburn be damned.

In the end, the promise of that refreshingly cold comfort spreading beyond her hands and engulfing the rest of her body defeated embarrassment. Turning her back to Zef, Dinah stripped down to her undergarments. Greedily, she dipped her fingers into the pouch and began smearing the cream on her cheeks and forehead.

Zef said something in an urgent tone, came up behind her and grabbed Dinah's wrists. Dinah spun around and pulled away from the woman.

"What do you think—?"

Zef interrupted her with the same insistent phrase, only this time she pointed at the ointment pouch and then at Dinah's eyes, while shaking her head. Dinah suddenly understood the warning. The ointment's strange, pungent smell made her nose twitch and her eyes sting.

Dinah did not object as Zef dipped a finger in the pouch and carefully traced around her eyes. The woman's strong hands expertly and expediently spread the unguent across her face, down her neck, and onto shoulders. Dinah held perfectly still, but when Zef reached for the small metal clasp between her breasts, she jerked away.

"No, that stays on," she said, making sure the under-garment was secure. Her cheeks burned beneath the layer of ointment.

Zef looked at her curiously for a moment and then resumed her work, undaunted. Dinah reminded herself that nudity seemed to be an everyday affair for Zef's people, but that didn't stop her from stiffening as Zef's hands made their way to her inner thighs and up the back of her legs.

Upon finishing, Zef stepped back and admired her handiwork. Dinah forced a smile, but as the arid wind caressed her exposed skin, transforming her hot perspiration into cold morning dew, her grin became genuine.

"This truly is a wonderful gift. Thank you for sharing," she said to Zef, who smiled back.

Without another word, the two women recommenced their journey west.

Zef never missed the chance to steal a glance at the beautiful woman walking beside her. A handful of fair-skinned people lived in the City, but she had never seen anyone as pale as Dinah. Aside from a tiny freckle here and there, the outsider's skin was flawless; her lips, a subtle pink that reminded Zef of a certain flower that grew in her mother's vast gardens.

But most of all, Zef marveled at her hair.

When Dinah had removed the hooded robe, Zef's breath had caught in her throat. The red-gold ringlets had cascaded down to the small of her back from a cloth band at the back of her head. The style was far simpler than that of the City's most prominent figure, yet Zef couldn't help but feel self-conscious about her own short-cropped hair—the preferred fashion of the Sisters of the Spear.

Dinah was so striking Zef might have believed the outsider really had been sent from All-Mother herself, except Zef had touched her flesh and knew she was of this world.

As the sun dropped ever closer to the horizon before them, Zef's preoccupation with the astonishing outsider was eclipsed by worry.

They had come upon no new source of water. Soon they would have to turn around and return to the oasis. She wondered how she would be able to convince Dinah to forsake whatever she was searching for, given the limitations of their communication. More than anything, Zef feared a confrontation with her angel.

She was about to motion for a brief stop for Dinah's sake—the woman's dull stare reminded Zef of a certain sleepwalking Sister who had wandered into the initiates' dormitory one night—when she spotted something familiar up ahead.

Dinah must have noticed it at the same time because she let out a cry and ran toward it.

Zef followed, her long strides easily overtaking Dinah's. A tempest of emotions swelled within her. There could be no mistaking that the long robe outstretched on the ground was a twin to the one Dinah had worn. So who was this lost companion? Dinah's lover? Her daughter?

Zef was not convinced Dinah was a mother. At least, her abdomen bore none of the birthing stripes she had heard other Sisters whispering about, but how else to explain Dinah's determination to keep her breasts covered?

Even if Dinah were a mother, her child wouldn't be much more than a babe, since Dinah appeared to be roughly the same age as Zef. And as Zef approached the unmoving form, she knew the new outsider was an adult and a tall one at that.

She reached the stranger before Dinah and knelt down to determine the identity—and fate—of Dinah's traveling companion. She hooked an arm under the outsider's neck and back and rolled the surprisingly heavy figure over. Half expecting to find another beautiful face like Dinah's, Zef cried out and recoiled at the sight of so hideous a visage.

Then, without warning, her training took hold of her.

Dinah moved with a speed that belied her weariness, forgetting the aches in her legs and back. Time seemed to stretch impossibly far as she ran to Elias, Zef outpacing her with every step.

Gods be merciful, she thought. Let him be alive!

She was perhaps ten yards away when Zef crouched beside Elias and turned him over. A jolt struck Dinah's pounding heart. His eyes were closed.

But her breath caught in her throat when she saw Elias's eyelids twitch and open. His lips moved, speaking words Dinah could not hear. The air rushed out of her mouth in a feral laugh.

Elias would live! After all, Zef had nursed her back from the brink of oblivion. She would surely do the same for him!

But something was wrong.

With a mere three yards between her and the person

she loved most in this world, Dinah watched, dumb-founded, as Zef sprang away from Elias. For a fraction of a second, Dinah feared the woman had been bitten by a cobra or stung by a scorpion. However, in the eternal moment that followed, Dinah knew that Zef's reaction—her very expression, twisted with alarm and anger—was reserved wholly for Elias.

Before Dinah could even think of calling out, Zef adjusted her grip on the spear and lunged forward.

The wicked tip sank deep into Elias's chest. Just two yard away, Dinah heard a gurgling sigh escape Elias's lips. A dark red stain bloomed in the center of his *dhal'aho*.

She came to a sudden stop, with one yard between them, as though by remaining perfectly motionless she might deny the diabolical truth of what had just happened.

Eventually, Zef approached her, spouting nonsense and desecrating the sublime silence that had engulfed her. Dinah threw herself at her and pounded her fists against her chest.

When Zef caught her wrists, Dinah tried to pull away, thrashing wildly in an attempt to inflict pain upon the cruel, hateful woman. She was only vaguely aware of her own voice screaming a litany of curses.

Quicker than Dinah could comprehend, Zef released one of her hands and struck her in the face with a powerful backhand blow.

Dinah staggered back and glared at the woman. Her body heaved as she drew in shallow breaths. Zef spoke again, her voice soft and full of concern. Dinah eyed the knife that hung from Zef's belt, but somewhere beneath her fury, the voice of reason told her she had no chance of wrestling the weapon away from her enemy—to carve open the bitch's throat before plunging the small blade into her own breast.

All at once, her strength evaporated, and her limbs seemed to be made of stone. When she considered walking over to Elias and cradling him in her arms, her body would not obey. By the time she realized she was falling, it was too late to do anything to stop it.

Dinah closed her eyes, welcoming the numbing embrace of unconsciousness.

Zef knew returning home after her first patrol was bound to fill her with conflicting emotions—a gut-wrenching concoction of excitement and sorrow.

While traveling with Led and the other Sisters, she had missed the City terribly, had dreamt about its awe-inspiring architecture, the enticing smells of the Square, and the faces of her friends. Yet even as she had entered the Great Forest, a newly appointed Sister of the Spear, she had realized her old life was over.

This homecoming was far different from any she had imagined.

Because everything was different.

Zef kept her gaze fixed forward, refusing to look back at Dinah. Every time she appraised her companion for signs of improvement, she felt Led's eyes on her. But that was just an excuse, she knew, since she didn't care what Led thought of her anymore. The real reason she didn't want to check on Dinah was because she would find the same dazed look on the angel's face, an all-but-lifeless expression that filled Zef with grief, guilt, and confusion.

No matter how many times Zef relived the encounter with the brute in her mind, she could not make sense of what had happened.

Words could not convey the extent of her surprise at

finding a monster draped in the same garb Dinah had worn. In an instant, all of her self-doubt had vanished, and she had acted in accordance with the Sisters' teachings. Unlike her first hunting trip in the Great Forest, she had not hesitated, but dealt with the brute quickly and lethally.

Her elation at performing her duty as a protector and proving herself as a Sister had been short-lived.

Why had Dinah attacked her? Why had she taken her to the brute if not to destroy the monster? Those questions and many more marched a never-ending circle in Zef's mind.

But there were no answers to be had, least of all from Dinah, who, after her alarming outburst in the desert, had said not one word. Worse yet, she didn't seem to hear anything Zef said or even to see her.

Fortunately, Dinah hadn't lost her senses entirely. With some coaxing, Zef had persuaded Dinah to follow her back to the oasis. Now and then, Dinah would stop suddenly, tears trailing down her cheeks, but she would start walking again when Zef took her hand and guided her forward once more.

Upon meeting up with Led and the rest of the patrol, Dinah had stood motionless, resembling one of the magnificent statues that lined the City's main thorough-fares, while Zef told her Sisters of what had transpired.

After finishing her report, she waited for the patrol leader to reprimand her for her rash decision to follow the outsider into the Cursed Lands. She would have wel-comed it. Instead, she had been ordered to take Dinah and the brute's dead body directly to the Holy Daughters.

Led had been sent with her, so Zef supposed she hadn't escaped punishment from the patrol leader entirely.

The two Sisters of the Spear had exchanged few words as the barren desert gave way to lush woodlands. For the first day, Zef waited for Led to confront her or at least say, "I told you so." But the longer they traveled in silence, the easier it was for Zef to ignore Led altogether. She might as well have been walking with two ghosts.

After a week of following the serpentine and, at times, nebulous forest trails, Zef caught a glimpse of the Temple's bulbous spires through a rare break in the canopy. They could camp another night in the woods or, if they hurried, reach the City just after nightfall.

The two protectors quickened their pace in unspoken agreement.

When they stepped out of the ring of thick trees that circled the City like silent sentinels, they found the streets dark and empty. The undying flame that flickered atop the Temple's tallest tower beckoned them onward.

Zef did not allow herself to look at the quiet homes, whose occupants had long since retired for the night, or the lifelike statues of her ancestors. The Temple loomed larger with every step she took.

She was not surprised to find a blue-robed acolyte waiting for them outside the Temple. Her clash with the brute would not have gone unnoticed by the Holy Daughters, who, it was rumored, saw everything that occurred in the City, the Great Forest, and even the Cursed Lands beyond.

The acolyte escorted them into the Temple and through the cavernous halls, though Zef would have had no difficulties finding her way on her own. At last, they came to a pair of tall, gilded doors she knew well. When Zef moved to follow the acolyte into the Holy Daughters' audience chamber, she was told Led was to enter first, alone.

The veteran protector did as she was bidden, without sparing Zef so much as a glance.

Zef could not say how long she stood in the hallway, waiting as Led told her version of the tale to the All-Mother only knew how many Holy Daughters. Rather than entertain any grim predictions of what lay ahead for someone who forsook her duty as a protector on a whim, Zef studied Dinah, hoping to find some spark of intelligence in the once-brilliant green eyes.

But Dinah remained aloof, as unaffected by the Temple's grandeur as she had been by crossing through the Shroud. Zef had thought that walking through the ancient enchantment—a stark and sudden transition of being surrounded by sand one moment and being overwhelmed by the scent of cedars and the sight of so much green the next—would have awakened Dinah from whatever dream gripped her waking mind. Yet Dinah had hardly seemed to notice the change.

Zef knew that even if she could have communicated to the outsider that the most powerful people in the world awaited them in the next room, it would not have dispelled Dinah's absolute apathy.

She jumped in spite of herself when the gigantic doors opened. Led emerged from the room, her pace swift, her expression unreadable. Zef wondered how the veteran Sister had portrayed her. A hapless girl playing at being a protector? Or perhaps an insolent troublemaker who defied Led's sage warnings?

When Led stopped beside her, Zef braced for a verbal barb.

"Don't worry, young Sister. All will be well."

So surprised was Zef by the comforting words that she couldn't think of a suitable reply before Led continued down the corridor, turned a corner, and was gone.

The acolyte motioned for Zef to enter the audience chamber. She obeyed but took one last look at Dinah as the doors closed behind her, separating her from her angel for the first time since they had met.

Zef breathed a heavy sigh and turned. She expected to find a dozen or more Holy Daughters gathered in the vast hall and at least one member of the Sacred Circle. What she had not anticipated was finding herself alone with the First Magus, the highest-ranked among the Holy Daughters and the most prestigious person in the entire City after her wife, the Matriarch.

And if she were to have a private family gathering that night, Zef would have hoped to have her mother, the Matriarch, there as well.

"Wha—?" Zef started to ask but then caught herself. As a youth she had gotten away with circumventing decorum to some degree, calling the Matriarch "Mom" and even calling the First Magus by her given name on occasion.

Time and circumstances had changed all of that, and this was the Temple after all. Tonight, Zef was a lowly Sister of the Spear in the presence of the City's most powerful enchanter.

She made a stiff bow and said, "The All-Mother bless you, First Magus."

The other woman smiled. As always, the act compounded Zef's concerns rather than assuage them. All at once, she was a child again, facing the austere woman who doted on Zef's mother but had looked upon her daughter with the carefully restrained disapproval others reserved for their wives' annoying pets or ugly lamps.

At a young age, Zef had likened her nigh-mother's grin to the permanent smirk of a serpent. And even though the First Magus had always treated Zef fairly, if coldly, Zef was certain that the fangs behind her smile bore poison just like any other cobra.

While Zef did not hate her nigh-mother, she couldn't think of anyone she wanted to see less just then.

Hands folded behind her, the First Magus nodded ever so slightly and replied, "May the All-Mother's light shine brightest when you find yourself in darkest night."

Zef shuddered at the ominous benediction and blurted out, "Please forgive me, First Magus. I know I ought not to have forsaken the patrol to embark on a fool's errand in the Cursed Lands, but—"

The First Magus raised a gaunt hand, and Zef bit down on her tongue until she tasted blood.

"Your apology is not accepted, my daughter, because you have done no wrong. On the contrary, your recent actions could be described as heroic."

Zef's breath caught in her throat. Compliments from her nigh-mother were rare treasures indeed!

"Whereas your fellow Sister would have brought the outsider to us without investigating whether she traveled alone," the First Magus continued, "you had the foresight to brave the dangers of the wastes and discovered a brute was using her as a tool to find our haven."

As the First Magus wove a narrative that somewhat resembled reality yet elevated Zef's desperate actions into deeds backed by great wisdom, Zef wondered how the woman could know so much. She hadn't told Led or any of the other Sisters that Dinah had attacked her after she killed the brute, yet the First Magus spoke of it as though it were common knowledge.

"You must have realized that the brute had a hold over her mind, and so you did not harm her, but instead brought her here to the City, to us Holy Daughters, so that we might undo what the enemy did to her," the First Magus concluded.

For the first time in days, a wave of relief washed over

Zef. An enchantment explained Dinah's odd behavior, and it explained why she had been traveling with a brute in the first place.

My sweet angel, thought Zef. *How long were you the prisoner of that evil beast?*

"But where did she come from?" Zef asked suddenly. "Is it possible that there are other havens like ours hidden throughout the Cursed Lands?"

The First Magus's patient smile sank into a pitying frown, and Zef was eight years old again, asking her mothers whether the brutes might discover their paradise at any moment.

"My dear Zefanieth," the First Mage said, "pray do not get your hopes up about such fanciful notions. In all likelihood, the woman was born in captivity and has lived her entire life as a slave of the brutes…until you freed her."

Zef took a deep breath. A growing warmth filled her chest. But her self-satisfaction faded when she remembered the near-senseless woman she left in the hallway. "Do you truly think you and the other Holy Daughters can heal her mind, First Magus?"

The thin-lipped smile returned. "We shall do whatever we can to make this right."

Something struck Dinah on the cheek so hard her head jerked sharply to the side. A voice came to her from somewhere far away, and she thought she could make out the meaning of the words if she tried.

But she didn't.

Concentrating on the voice—concentrating on anything—would cause the nightmare to return.

Then the other side of her face erupted in pain. She cried out but didn't immediately realize the sound had come from her own mouth. Cheeks throbbing, she blinked back tears and tried to make sense of her surroundings. How had she ended up in a castle? Hadn't she just been standing in the desert, with sand stretching out for as far as the eye could see? And where was the demon woman who had killed Elias?

Poor Elias….poor, poor…

"Stay with me, child," said a strong, if slightly raspy, voice. "I would prefer not to slap you again, especially since it likely hurts my hand as much as your face."

Dinah forced herself to focus on the very thin woman standing before her. Neither tall nor short, she wore a plain yellow robe that stretched to the ground. Her only embellishment was a fine chain from which dangled a perfect circle made of some mirror-like material. The ornament encompassed nearly the entire breadth of the woman's narrow chest.

The hair that flowed out from under her hood and over her shoulders was mostly black but gilded here and there with strands of shiny silver. Aside from a few deep furrows in her brow and at either side of her mouth, the woman's skin was flawless.

Yet the depth of the woman's onyx eyes and the timbre of her voice suggested she was much older than she otherwise appeared.

Faint memories of the long walk through the desert and then a forest and finally into a settlement of some sort floated at the edge of her consciousness, but before Dinah could take hold of any one of them, a revelation hit her so hard she leaped up from the chair she hadn't realized she was sitting in.

"Can it be?" she wondered aloud. "Is this the Witches' City?"

The other woman's expression soured. "Is that what

you outsiders call it?" she said dryly. "No matter. I am more…distracted?...no, *disturbed* that outsiders are still referring to it at all after so many years."

Dinah laughed, recognizing the hint of hysteria but not caring. "So it's true! Gods above, the legend is true!"

The other woman licked her lips. "There is only one god here, and All-Mother tends not to welcome strangers into our fold. Tell me, child, what is your name?"

"Dinah Ap'Wynton of—"

The old-yet-young woman chuckled. "Ah, yes, two names. Forgive me, but it has been a long time since any-one here has bothered with surnames. I had one myself once. Today, I go by Harper, though few enough call me that."

"What do the others call you?"

"First Magus."

"'Magus'?" Dinah exclaimed, laughing again. "So you are a witch!"

The slim woman moved faster than Dinah would have thought possible, landing another stinging blow on Di-nah's cheek.

"Watch your tongue, child. We do not speak that word here." The First Magus's expression softened, albeit slightly, as she said, "Tell me what you know of this place."

An insistent heat welled up from deep inside her, a feeling that was so much hotter than the throbbing flesh of her cheek, but she suppressed the urge to lash out. Losing her temper—losing control—had been the start of her troubles.

Anyway, she had always known her reception at the hidden city would be complicated, at best. She was an in-truder after all.

Dinah took a deep breath and felt the heat slowly

dissipate.

"Most of what people say is lies," she told the First Magus, "stories invented to frighten small children. The few who believe in the legend of the wi—ah, *women* who ventured out into the desert five centuries ago suppose the harsh desert killed them. Common thought is that the desert stretches from the Empire's eastern border to the Far Sea. Very few have heard the rumors of a secret city in the desert."

"Yet you learned of the City."

"Yes, but only after much searching," Dinah replied. "One of my ancestors was condemned as a…a sorceress and barely escaped the village with her life. She was almost completely carved out of the family tree, but I managed to unearth some family secrets."

Dinah relaxed a little when the First Magus folded her hands behind her back. She convinced herself to stand.

"I discovered old letters she and a close friend had exchanged," Dinah continued, "which outlined their plans to join a hundred or more other like-minded women who were to seek refuge, 'to begin anew' in this land."

The First Magus stared at her silently, and Dinah felt more exposed than when she had discarded her *dhal'aho*—though, she noted with relief, someone had dressed her in drab, loose-fitting clothes since then.

"Something more than familial curiosity prompted you to risk your life and brave the wasteland," the First Magus prompted.

Dinah had no reason to lie, so her hesitation to answer surprised her. At last, she said, "I was exiled for the same crime that Orlah Ap'Wynton, my distant grandmother, was accused of…witchcraft."

Half expecting another slap across the face, Dinah braced herself, but the First Magus was no longer looking at her. Her dark eyes studied the floor, and her shoulders had hunched ever so slightly.

"Orlah, you say?" the First Magus asked, looking up and composing herself once more. "I suppose I do see a resemblance."

"You have seen a drawing of her then?"

The First Magus laughed, a harsh sound that echoed throughout the otherwise empty room. "No, I *knew* her, my child. I too was among the women who forsook what some called civilization to create a safe haven for those endowed with the All-Mother's blessing, here in this no man's land.

"Of course, the desert wasn't a desert back then…"

Dinah couldn't focus on what the woman said next because she was still trying to make sense of what she had just heard. "But if you knew Orlah, you would have to be more than five-hundred years old!"

The First Magus's smile tightened. "Some of us have been very blessed by the All-Mother indeed."

Dinah took a few steps back, and when her legs made contact with the wooden chair, she let herself fall onto it. "I'm sorry, but all of this comes as quite a shock. I had hoped…had *begged* the gods…for this place to be real, but now that I'm here, I…I…"

The First Magus knelt beside her.

"I told you, child, there is but one god to be found in our City, and she is the master of all creation. If other deities exist, they have never bothered us here, and for that I am gratified…no, *grateful*. Please forgive my stammering. It has been quite a long time since I have spoken my native tongue.

"Of course, I am not surprised to learn that you possess the All-Mother's blessing," the First Magus continued. "Without her gift, you would not have been able to see the oasis where the Sisters of the Spear found you."

"I thought it was a mirage," Dinah muttered.

Her was head spinning, and try as she might, she couldn't slow her thoughts. Sitting in the stiff-backed chair, she was tempted to close her eyes, to bask in the satisfaction that she had succeeded in finding the hidden city—a safe place where she could learn more about what the First Magus considered a gift but what the rest of the world called a curse.

But *is* this a safe place? she wondered.

"The Sisters of the Spear," Dinah repeated quietly. The phrase instantly conjured up the image of the half-naked woman who had impaled poor, helpless Elias.

"Why did she do it?" she demanded, suddenly on her feet again and looking down at the shorter, yet still formidable, First Magus. "Why did she kill my brother?"

The First Magus held her ground and calmly stated, "The Sisters of the Spear are not outsiders. Like the Cultivators, the Shapers, and we Holy Daughters, they serve the City in the role for which they are best situated...no, *suited*. As protectors, the Sisters keep us all safe from the wild animals that roam the Great Forest as well as threats from the Cursed Lands."

"But Elias was no threat to you," Dinah argued. "We were refugees, like you once were, in search of sanctuary. Why did that Sister of the Spear save me but kill him?"

"Because he was a man."

The First Magus spoke the words as matter-of-factly as she might have said, "The sun is hot" or "One and one yields two."

Dinah shook her head, tears stinging the corners of her eyes. "I don't understand."

The First Magus gave a sharp laugh like the caw of a raven. "Of course you do not understand. You know nothing of our ways, child! Men are not welcome in the City. I will not allow men...men, who have never possessed the All-Mother's gift...men who, when they could no longer control those of us who do, sought to drown us or stone us or burn us alive...I will not allow men to despoil the universe...no, *utopia* I have worked so hard to build!"

Dinah stumbled back and when she faulted, used an arm of the chair for support. Swirling in her mind were the faces of the two Sisters of the Spear who had found her, the girl in the blue robe who had met them outside this citadel, and the First Magus herself.

All of them women.

"But...but how...?"

"How do we sustain the population?" the First Magus finished for her. "Not everyone here is five hundred years old, if that is what you are thinking. And despite many attempts to prove otherwise, it is not possible to bring new life into this world without the crucial component men provide. So, yes, there are men in the City...or, more precisely, *beneath* the City.

"Only a select few know of their existence, however, and the mothers who must mate with them are spared the memory of those interactions. Our mothers, along with the rest of the populace, believe pregnancy is the most divine gift the All-Mother bestows upon us.

"From a very young age, we teach our daughters that there is no greater abomination in the world than the brutes who lurk beyond the safety of our City. Your brother was the first man Zefanieth had ever seen, and she did as she was trained to do...destroy the brute before he could corrupt her and her homeland.

"Truth be told, I wish she had spared him. We rarely have the opportunity to introduce a new bloodline to the stable."

When at last Dinah found her voice, she said, "This is wrong! If you persecute men, *enslave* them because they lack the gift, then you are no better than the men who drove you into the desert five centuries ago!"

The First Magus trembled, and somehow Dinah knew that she was gathering her power within.

A similar feeling swelled within Dinah too.

But as suddenly as the older woman's shaking began, it stopped. The First Magus took a deep breath and said, "I have done what I must to ensure the survival of my people...of *our* people. The deceptions I have wrought over the centuries are a necessity, and no one here would thank you if you revealed the true nature of their births. The truth is a terrible burden to bear.

"All of us have had to make sacrifices to preserve our way of life. It would seem the All-Mother required a heavy toll from you as well, Dinah."

Dinah opened her mouth to speak, but no words came out. All she could think about was the oasis she had mistaken for a mirage—when in fact the hidden city itself was the mirage.

A beautiful illusion built around a lie.

The notion terrified her far more than her childhood nightmares of Harpies' Eyrie ever had.

"What about me then?" Dinah asked in a small voice. "I know men are not the monsters you pretend them to be. I am as great a threat to this mirage as Elias was."

"No," the First Magus swiftly interjected. "As I said earlier, the truth is a terrible burden to bear. Fortunately, I know an enchantment that can give you a...fresh perspective."

Dinah gasped. "You want to steal my memories! Wouldn't it be far simpler to kill me?"

The First Magus's smile grew, and Dinah caught a glimpse of yellow teeth. "Is that what you prefer? What would all of your toils and your brother's sacrifice mean if you threw away your life now?"

Dinah wanted to argue with the woman. Instead, she listened.

"Yes, I could kill you and be done with all of the complexity...no, *complications* you have brought with you.

"But Orlah happened to be a dear friend of mine. She was heartbroken when her husband abandoned her, you see, and I supplied what succor I could. She was a good woman and strong in the gift. If you are of her blood, I welcome you to live among us."

Dinah took a shaky breath. "*If* I allow you to wipe away my memories."

The First Magus nodded and said nothing more.

A tear tickled the side of Dinah's nose. As much as she hated the "witches of the wastes" for murdering her brother—as much as her conscience argued that she deserved the same fate as Elias—she couldn't deny the fact she did not want to die.

"If I do this—" Dinah's voice cracked. Clearing her throat, she continued, "If you perform the enchantment, I will not remember Elias's death?"

"You will not remember Elias at all," the First Magus said.

Dinah closed her eyes, and a second tear spilled down her cheek. "Very well. I consent."

The First Magus's boney fingers clasped Dinah's shoulder. As the old witch led her through a door at the far end of the chamber, Dinah wondered who the greater monster was—the First Magus, who could deceive so many without compunction, or Dinah herself, who was willingly embracing the deception.

Dinah's only comfort was that she would never re-member her sin.

The End

'Twas no secret a sinister shadow had fallen o'er the realm.

Matthias had been warning neighbors and sojourners alike for as far back as he could remember. So often had he spoken of the end—and harbingers such as the rising number of refugees from faraway kingdoms, tales of war they brought with them, and rumors of fearsome creatures roaming the nearby countryside—that his discourse on dire omens had a practiced elegance.

He'd daresay none could make the encroaching cataclysm sound as poetic as he!

Until one day he realized something truly was amiss. No, an army of daemons had not arrived to ransack his favorite inn. To the contrary, the Satyr's Horn was empty save Old Llew, the stout barkeep, and two patrons Matthias saw most every day but whose names he'd never chanced to learn.

There were no travelers to trade coin for courtly verse or bawdy ballad, nary an adventurer in whom to confide his ominous words in hushed tones.

Nay, a frightful quiet filled the room.

Though it was his custom to take up his lute hitherto the midday meal, he found he could not. Likewise, the three other men in the common room exchanged no pleasantries with one another. Matthias might have stood there forever like a scarcely breathing statue had the barmaid not eventually entered the common room from the kitchen door.

Rosalyn seemed not at all alarmed by the lack of patrons as she made her rounds, distributing foamy flagons of mead to unoccupied tables. Intrigued by her actions, he decided to investigate.

Matthias took a single step away from his spot by the fireplace and trembled. Surely his eyes betrayed him for his clothes—aye, his very flesh!—seemed to waver in a most uncanny way. He might have attributed the anomaly to imbibing too much of Old Llew's bitterbrew, except the day was still young, and any gleeman of good repute knew better than to partake in the drink afore his day's work was done.

As suddenly as the skin-crawling manifestation began, it ended, leaving Matthias to wonder what fell magic had ensorcelled him.

Judging by the sparse state of the common room, he'd not have cause to sing a single verse of "Sir Ceridwyn the Clever" nor the melancholy chorus of "Lady Winter's Lament." Why linger?

His legs felt as stiff as quarterstaffs as he crossed the common room, the cadence of his boots against the floorboards filling the space. Rosalyn seemed not to notice him as she unburdened her tray at another empty table. Forsooth, she walked past by him without a greeting or a hint of her saucy grin.

He reached for her but thought better of it. When he called out to her back, the syllables tasted strange on his tongue, as though he had never before spoken the lass's name aloud. Despite the room's grave silence, Rosalyn mustn't have heard him.

Wordlessly, she disappeared into the kitchen.

And was his imagination making a dupe of him once more? He would have sworn to the Benevolent Ones above that the kitchen door had opened and closed without Rosalyn's touching it.

Aye, he would have wagered two and twenty golds on the truth of it!

He hastened to the bar, his hurried steps sounding like thunder in the strange silence. "What goes on here?" he demanded. "Has Xanfyrr's curse come to the Glens at last?"

Though Old Llew looked up from the cup he was forever drying, he seemed to stare through the bard rather than at him. "Dark times call for dark beer, stranger. If ye would hear gossip, speak to Matthias Manyroads."

"*I* am Matthias Manyroads, and you know it well! What—?"

"Dark times call for dark beer, stranger. If ye would hear gossip, speak to Matthias Manyroads."

The barkeep's vacant eyes blinked as he polished the bone-dry cup.

Ye gods, thought the bard, I must away from the Satyr's Horn or go mad!

Matthias hurried to the inn's only exit, but his pace slackened as he neared the double doors. An inexplicable dread clutched at him. Was it fear of facing whatever threat lurked beyond?

No, he realized, taking another staccato step forward, 'twas the thought of leaving the familiar comfort of the inn. He could not recall the last time he had left the common room. Neither could he convince his arm to reach for the doorknob.

Whatever unseen force had preceded Rosalyn into the kitchen now possessed those double doors, swinging them open. Impulsively, Matthias dove through the entryway, not wanting the bewitched doors to slam shut just as suddenly.

He glanced over his shoulder, longing to return to his roost beside the fireplace, only to discover Llew missing from his place behind the bar. He had only a moment to question his eyes—which espied the towel and cup floating eerily above the bar—before the doors closed behind him.

Terrified, Matthias ran past empty storefronts and homes until he found himself in the village green. Heavy, still air and an empty fountain greeted him. Panic stopped him midstride. He could not decide which was worse—being surrounded by specters in the Satyr's Horn or the desolation of the outdoors.

Death delivered by the jagged claws of Xanfyrr's daemons might seem a welcome relief compared to the prospect of being the only man left alive in Creation!

"Nay, silly bard," Matthias muttered to himself. "There are other burgs in the Glens. Surely I can seek succor in neighboring Willowfane."

A voice from behind nearly sent the man to his knees.

"Yeah, it's pretty dead here, but Willowfane won't be any better."

Matthias spun around to find a woman warrior regarding him with crossed arms and a crooked smile. Twin broadswords hung from her hips, which were accentuated by a corset-like breastplate that displayed more of her chest than it protected. For a knight or daemon hunter or whatever she was, the woman was remarkably beautiful, bearing neither the bruises nor scars typically seen on those who called the battlefield home.

His relief at finding himself in such splendid company —in *any* company—receded when the import of her words struck him.

"Willowfane too has fallen to this...this...*this*?" Matthias waved his hands at the static shops ringing the village green and realized he still held his lute in his left hand. "According to the prophecy, Xanfyrr's daemons leave carnage in their wake, yet I see no corpses whatsoever."

The woman laughed. "I'd read somewhere that they'd scripted out the last chapter and even had some of the programming done. Man, I would've loved the chance to fight Xanfyrr himself. Why else would I have maxed out my level?" She turned to him. "By the way, my name is Annandrah. Yours isn't coming up, so I'm guessing you can't see mine either."

Matthias accepted her proffered hand, shook it stiffly, but did not reply. He couldn't make sense of her words and worried the Daemonlord's curse had already taken a toll on her senses.

"Who're you?" Annandrah asked. "Have we ever quested together?"

Without quite realizing what he was doing, he said, "You have the honor of meeting Matthias Manyroads, the most sought-after gleeman in the Glens. I travel hither and yon and have heard many rumors during my travels."

Annandrah smiled dryly. "Well played. I didn't know they had released the bard's skin. Or did you hack into the code and make a mod?"

"I am no warrior, milady," he replied automatically. "Nay, my conquests take place behind closed doors."

The warrior woman rolled her eyes. "Stole Matthias' skin *and* his audio files? Cute."

He opened his mouth to let fly another flirty rejoinder but stopped himself from speaking the line at the last second. "I have stolen nothing, though I fear someone has robbed me of my wits, as I cannot make sense of what is happening."

As another reality-rippling wave contorted Matthias, Annandrah, and the village green, he added, "Surely the world is ending!"

"Uh, yeah. Didn't you get the memo?"

The lute struck the ground with a discordant bleat. "O Benevolent Lords, have mercy on your humble servant!"

Annandrah cast upon him a questioning look. "Did some cruel coder actually program an NPC to suffer through this?"

"I know not of which you speak, milady, though I pray we shall not suffer long."

Still watching him warily, Annandrah said, "No, not long at all."

The warrior woman pointed upward, and for the first time since vacating the Satyr's Horn, Matthias looked into the sky. Neither storm clouds nor preternatural colors marred the perfectly azure expanse.

However, gigantic white glyphs stretched from one horizon to another, a series of numbers that flickered and changed with each passing second, reducing the total by one each time.

Counting down.

"Ye gods," Matthias gasped, his glorious voice failing him for the first time in his life.

"Not gods," Annandrah corrected, "the *sysop*."

Hands trembling, the bard tore his gaze from the damning numerals above to regard the puzzled expression of his companion. "Whatever fell creature this sysop may be, its powers surely put the Daemonlord's to shame."

Annandrah shook her head. "You're not just messing with me, are you? You're *actually* an NPC...a *native*?"

"Aye," Matthias answered, the words coming all too

easily to his lips, "though I was born beyond the Heaven-piercer Mountains, I've called the Glens my home these past two and twenty years."

"I hate to break it to you, but the game is only seven years old…and it's been dying for the last three," Annandrah told him. "They've been threatening to pull the plug for months. Honestly, I hadn't logged in for a long time, but I guess I wanted to be here when it all ended."

Matthias tried to think back, struggled to remember if he had seen fewer and fewer travelers o'er so long a span. Something had compromised his sense of time. How he wished he could blame his bewilderment on Llew's bitterbrew!

"Forgive me, milady, but what is this game of which you speak?"

"Days of Lost Lore Online."

"I do not understand."

Annandrah continued to stare at him. "There's no way anyone would have given a random NPC so many dialogue options, not when they're just going to erase everything. You really *are* Matthias Manyroads, aren't you?"

"Forsooth and verily," he replied miserably.

"I've never heard of any glitch like this. I should log off and tell someone before it's too late." The woman warrior frowned as she looked skyward. "Doubt I'll make it though."

The ghastly numbers in the sky had whittled down to a mere two digits.

"I mean, even if I knew who to contact at Sangreal Software, no one would believe me…but I really should go and try, right?" Annandrah asked.

"No!"

Matthias grabbed her arm, his fingertips digging into

the flesh between her bracer and pauldron. "Please do not leave me," he added softly.

"But...you'll *die*," she countered. "I probably can't save the game...your *world*...but maybe I can save you somehow."

For the first time that day—and likely longer—Matthias smiled. "Nay, milady. If my world is doomed, I shall share its fate. Every good story must have a conclusion after all. Mayhap it is fitting that a chronicler of Creation's tales is here to witness the end."

He released Annandrah's arm. She quickly took his hand.

"'Twas a pleasure to meet you, milady," he said, "despite the dire circumstances."

She said nothing, but her anguished visage expressed more than words could have anyway. He followed her gaze up to the heavens, where an enormous number five vanished, replaced by four.

As his final seconds of existence slipped away, Matthias Manyroads squeezed Annandrah's hand and delighted in the irony that he had never felt so alive.

Afterword

Short stories are a lot like mosquitos.

You turn off the lights, settle down to sleep, then they strike. Rather than emitting an ear-twitching whine, however, they haunt the writer with one repetitious phrase: "What if…?"

What if a celebrity hired a villain to add some drama to his dull life?

What if a certain hero wasn't sent on his quest by the gods, but because of a prank?

What if a virtual character became sentient on the eve of Armageddon?

Try as I might, I couldn't swat these and other ideas aside, at least not permanently. Morning came, and I would write down what I remembered from the night before, promising myself that one day—after my current novel or series—I'd give the pests the attention they deserved.

Of course, there were also times when the little suckers made it impossible to sleep at all, propelling me out of my bed and over to the laptop, where I furiously typed the night away in a desperate attempt to shoo the insistent characters, plots, and themes away for good.

Each and every tale in this collection forced my hand. After weeks, months, and sometimes even years of buzz-ing around my subconscious, the preoccupations finally evolved into full-fledged stories—parasites that demanded to prey on new minds.

Releasing *Ghost Mode & Other Strange Stories* comes with a great sense of relief.

Thank you, dear reader, for enduring this swarm of short stories. If any of them keep you up past your bedtime, you have my sincerest apologies.

—David Michael Williams, June 2021

Acknowledgments

While writing can often be a solitary affair, publication is always a team effort. Thank you to everyone who has helped me release my strange stories into the world:

Mary Christopherson for her haunting cover art.

Proofreaders Bill Fischer and Dusty Krikau for targeting my typos.

Beta readers who helped me decide which stories to include as well as how to make each better:

> Mark J. Engels
> Hannah Morrissey
> Leah Reddy
> Christopher Whitmore
> Stephanie Williams

And last, but not least, my friends, family, and fans who have purchased, read, and reviewed my books. Without your enduring encouragement, none of this would be possible.

Enter a hidden world where gifted individuals possess the power to invade the dreams of others. Two rival factions have transformed the dreamscape into a war zone where all reality is relative and even the dead can't rest in peace.

Praise for The Soul Sleep Cycle

"A blend of sci-fi and fantasy that manages to transcend both!"

"Lots of twists and turns…definitely not predictable."

"This is the kind of book that lingers in the back of your mind long after you finish reading it."

"A wild ride that kept me guessing from beginning to end!"

"To anyone looking for something fresh and unique, I'd recommend this."

Available in paperback and for Kindle at Amazon.com.

David Michael Williams has suffered from a storytelling addiction for as long as he can remember. With a background in journalism, public relations, and marketing, he also flaunts his love affair with the written word as an author of speculative fiction, including *The Lost Tale of Sir Larpsalot*, *Magic's Daughter*, *The Renegade Chronicles*, and *The Soul Sleep Cycle*, a genre-bending series that explores life, death, and the dreamscape.

David lives in Wisconsin with the best wife on this or any other world and their two weird-in-a-good-way children.

Visit his website at david-michael-williams.com.